Intimate possession

Georgina gasped. "What a nerve. I don't belong to you, Mr. Leon Alexander, not now, not ever."

His hands came down heavily on her shoulders. "If I were you, Miss Georgina Gregory, I wouldn't be too sure about that. When I make up my mind about something I rarely change it."

She swallowed hard and met the cool grayness of his eyes. "I think you're underestimating me. I'm a free agent. No one owns me, least of all you."

The corners of his mouth lifted. "Your fighting spirit is what I like best. But you're mine, Georgina, mine until I consider I've had fair recompense for the money Craig took." His fingers moved beneath the heavy fall of her hair, reaching for her nape, his thumbs stroking the soft skin behind her ears.

Margaret Mayo began writing quite by chance when the engineering company she worked for wasn't very busy and she found herself with time on her hands. Today, with more than thirty romance novels to her credit, she admits that writing governs her life to a large extent. When she and her husband holiday—Cornwall is their favorite spot— Margaret always has a notebook and camera on hand and is constantly looking for fresh ideas. She lives in the countryside near Stafford, England.

Books by Margaret Mayo

Don't miss any of our special offers. Write to us at the following address for information on our newest releases.

Harlequin Reader Service
P.O. Box 1397, Buffalo, NY 14240
Canadian address: P.O. Box 603,
Fort Erie, Ont. L2A 5X3

MARGARET MAYO

A Fiery Encounter

Harlequin Books

TORONTO • NEW YORK • LONDON
AMSTERDAM • PARIS • SYDNEY • HAMBURG
STOCKHOLM • ATHENS • TOKYO • MILAN
MADRID • WARSAW • BUDAPEST • AUCKLAND

Harlequin Presents first edition January 1993
ISBN 0-373-11525-3

Original hardcover edition published in 1991
by Mills & Boon Limited

A FIERY ENCOUNTER

CHAPTER ONE

'THERE'S Leon Alexander.' Helen nudged Georgina and pointed. There was no missing him. He stood out from the crowd like a king among men. He was tall, taller than anyone else present, his hair thick and black with silver threads running through it, his face all chiselled angles. He had a wide mouth, and, when he smiled, which he did at this moment, his teeth were large; Helen said he actually snapped them at people.

The thought made Georgina smile. She had this picture-image of him taking a bite out of someone's arm—and just at that moment his eyes caught hers. A very brief moment, a flicker, then his attention was turned back to the group of people he was with. But in that infinitely short space of time Georgina felt some of his power.

He certainly did not look like an ogre, he did not look as though he cracked the whip to drive his work-force harder. 'He's nothing like I imagined,' she said in a low tone to her friend. 'He's gorgeous.' She had dressed carefully for this cocktail party in a short silver dress with a deep V back and front. It was ruched around her hips and fitted her slender figure as though it had been made for her.

She had left her long hair loose, framing her face in a cloud of fiery chestnut waves and curls. She rarely wore make-up but tonight she had emphasised her eyes with grey shadow and lashings of mascara, and wore a bronzy lipstick that did not clash with her hair.

An antique silver locket hung from its chain in the hollow between her breasts; other than that she wore no jewellery. Georgina was tall and graceful and held herself well and tonight she looked stunning.

'Leon's looks belie the man underneath,' hissed Helen, who was smaller than her friend and not so pretty, with short dark hair and laughing blue eyes. 'Believe me, I know from personal experience.'

Georgina was aware of Helen's bitterness but felt sure it was overdone. As they moved around the room, drawing nearer to this man who was the new owner of the company for whom her friend worked, she could hear the low growl of his voice. It had an unusual timbre that set her teeth on edge. Helen had said nothing about his voice! It was the sort of voice that thrilled to the core and, judging by the rapt expression on the faces of the women who were listening to him, she wasn't the only one to feel that way.

They were near enough now to hear what he was saying. '... Involves a great deal of hard work but hard work never hurt anyone.'

It really was an unforgettable voice, deeper than any she had ever heard. You could hear this man talking and know instantly it was he without even seeing him. It was a sexy voice, and she could imagine him whispering words of love, but it wouldn't be a whisper, it would still be that deep, toe-curling growl. Georgina shivered.

'If any of you are interested, come to my office tomorrow morning.'

There was a murmur of assent and the group broke up. Georgina and Helen were right behind him now, but when Helen wandered away to speak to one of her colleagues Georgina remained rooted to the spot, unable to take her eyes off him. He had wide shoulders and narrow hips, and she could guess at the powerful muscles beneath the immaculate cut of his dinner suit. For some unknown reason her heart began to race. He exuded a chemistry she could not ignore. It hung over him like an aura and she did not realise that she was staring until he suddenly turned.

She felt for the first time the full impact of his steel-grey eyes. He smiled, that wolfish smile Helen had told her about, and the air about her thickened so that she could not breathe. 'I don't believe we've had the pleasure?'

'Georgina Gregory,' she answered without hesitation.

He took her hand and his grip was firm—and earth-shaking! Georgina felt her pulse spin into overtime. 'A nice name,' he complimented in his low, distinctive growl. 'Do you work for the company? But no, of course not, I would most certainly remember seeing someone as beautiful as you.'

And he was the type of man no woman would forget either. He was unbelievably handsome, and so charming! Helen couldn't have been speaking the truth when she said he was arrogant and rude.

'Who are you with?' He glanced at her hand to see whether she wore a ring and Georgina thought she saw a flicker of pleasure in his eyes, but of course it could have been imagination. He was definitely all male, a raw, full-blooded male, who turned her bones to jelly and her blood to water.

'Helen Chapman.'

'Ah, yes, Helen.' His eyes narrowed as he looked at her friend, who was still talking to another girl and was completely unaware of what was going on. 'I hope you're enjoying yourself?' His question was the normal polite thing any host would ask, but his tone and the sexy timbre of it made it sound as though he really meant what he said, as though he genuinely wanted her to have a good time.

Her smile was brilliant. 'It's a marvellous party.'

'I always believe in getting to know my employees and their husbands and wives personally. A party like this provides an excellent opportunity. Helen, of course, being single, has brought her friend. A bonus as far as I'm concerned, Georgina. You're by far the most attractive girl here tonight. And your hair, it's so striking, I noticed you the moment you walked into the room. It's like a fire, it's beautiful. Have you a temper to match?'

Georgina grinned and shook her head. 'Not often, anyway.'

'I like girls with spirit.'

And I like men who know how to make a girl feel feminine and sexy, she answered silently.

'I think a toast to you, Georgina with the beautiful hair.' He raised his glass, his smile all-encompassing, sending more and more currents of sensation through her, but his smile changed to alarm when he was jostled from behind and before he could stop himself he had spilt his drink down the front of Georgina's expensive new dress.

'Oh, lord, I'm sorry, I'm terribly sorry.' Leon Alexander could not apologise quickly enough, concern in his steel-grey eyes, a handkerchief whipped out of his pocket and pushed into her hand.

Georgina dabbed ineffectually at the spreading red stain which covered one breast and dripped down inside her dress to her navel.

'Georgina, what can I say?' His eyes were dark and troubled. 'Your dress is ruined. How could I have been so clumsy?'

'No, please, it doesn't matter,' she said quickly, smiling up at him and catching her breath. He really was incredibly good-looking. 'It was an accident, it wasn't your fault. I'm sure it will clean.'

The commotion had attracted attention and Helen came swiftly to Georgina's side. 'What's happened?' Then she gasped as she saw the purplish-red stain. 'Oh, dear.'

'It's all right,' smiled Georgina, 'it's nothing to worry about. Someone bumped into Mr Alexander; he couldn't help it.'

Helen frowned, as if wondering what Georgina was doing talking to Leon Alexander anyway.

'I'll take you home so that you can change,' said Leon softly in Georgina's ear, his hand on her elbow, urging her through the throng of people.

Helen hurried after them. 'Georgina, where are you going?'

'Home to change.'

'But I can take you. There's no need for Mr Alexander to leave his party.'

'It's the very least I can do,' he insisted. 'You stay and enjoy yourself, Helen.'

She clearly did not like it and Georgina guessed it was sour grapes. Helen had had a crush on him when he first took over Puter Software and had done her best to try and make him notice her. She had been hurt and humiliated when he rebuffed her and now never lost an opportunity to run him down.

He drove a Ferrari, a fierce black monster that roared and growled in exactly the same way Helen claimed he did. Georgina had seen none of it yet and wondered whether her friend was exaggerating. As far as she was concerned he exuded charm out of every pore; he was looking across at her constantly to reassure himself that she was all right.

She was intensely conscious of him, her whole body throbbing in response to his male sensuality, smiling when their eyes met, feeling flattered that he was paying her so much attention. She knew, though, that she had to be careful not to read too much into it. Helen said that he dated many girls but took none of them seriously.

Georgina's flat was at the top of a big old house, and there was no lift. Leon Alexander carefully slowed his steps to match hers, but she imagined that on his own he would have bounded up two at a time. And so would she! But tonight she was a lady.

Her flat with its mixture of old and new furniture was clean and tidy, and was she glad! Often she left things lying all over the place. 'Please sit down,' she said. 'Make yourself comfortable. I'll try not to be long.'

'There's no rush at all,' he told her with his all-encompassing smile that set every one of her nerves tingling. A rush of apprehension overcame her. She knew nothing about this man except what Helen had told her—and that had been distinctly unflattering. Was she safe with him? Had it been wise to accept his offer? Was she about to become another statistic?

It wasn't until she had slipped out of her dress that she realised it wasn't simply a matter of changing. She needed a shower. And to reach the bathroom she had to go back through the living-room!

Self-consciously she opened the door, her short towelling robe belted tightly around her waist. 'I'm sorry—I'll have to shower, I'm in a worse mess than I thought. Put some music on if you like, and there's some whisky in that cupboard.'

'You don't have to apologise,' he said, 'when the whole thing's my fault.' His eyes flickered briefly over the full length of her legs, and he knew she was naked beneath the robe. Georgina grew warm and wondered what she was doing letting a total stranger see her like this. She slid quickly into the bathroom.

Beneath the jets she thought about Leon Alexander. He didn't actually feel like a stranger. Helen had told her so much about him that she felt she knew him already, and yet Helen's claims didn't altogether add up. She had been right about him being good-looking; he was an extremely attractive man. Not handsome in the true sense of the word, but with a charisma that could not be ignored. But arrogant, hard, condescending? He was none of these things—unless the charm was turned on especially for her benefit? 'All he needs is a whip,' Helen had said. Surely that wasn't true? She could not imagine him treating his workers like that.

By the time she had finished showering Georgina was humming contentedly. She had a zest for living that was not very much dampened, and tonight, despite her ruined dress, she was happy. Very happy. Her cheeks were pink, her hair curling tightly, and Leon Alexander looked up at her with a smile when she crossed the room.

'Do you feel better?'

'Much. I won't be long now. You must be anxious to get back to your party. Everyone will be wondering what has happened to you.' Her awareness of him was increasing by the second, or was it her nakedness? It was positively indecent standing like this in front of a man she barely knew. Wait till she told Helen! Her friend would be green with jealousy.

With a self-conscious smile she re-entered her bedroom and closed the door. She surveyed the contents of her wardrobe and decided on the white silk. The soft material was gathered into a wide band around her neck, leaving her shoulders bare. She fastened a thin gilt chain around her waist and slid her feet into gold, high-heeled sandals. She ran a wide-toothed comb through her hair, hardly disturbing the damp curls, and let herself back into the living-room.

He stood immediately and made a long, slow, deliberate appraisal. Every one of her pulses responded. He missed not an inch of her body, telling her without words that he found her desirable. Her heart thudded against her ribcage and she marvelled that such an obviously attractive man was not married. Was he too choosy? Was he still waiting for the right girl? Rumour had it, according to Helen, that he'd had a bad experience somewhere along the line—and yet it hadn't put him off women—quite the contrary.

'What can I say?' He spread his hands in a gesture of defeat. 'I thought you were beautiful before—now you're stunning. Quite stunning. I don't think we should go back to the party, do you? I think I should take you out somewhere to dinner.'

Georgina gasped. The thought was definitely appealing. 'But your guests... You said this party was so that you could get to know them personally.'

'Which I've already done,' he told her easily, and in a much lower growl, 'I think dinner with you will be much more exciting.'

And so did she. She allowed a tiny smile, holding back the huge grin. 'Actually I am hungry. Those bits and pieces didn't fill my hollow tooth.'

His mouth twitched. 'I agree. Let's get some real food inside ourselves.'

Her heart drummed a tattoo as she sat beside him in his car. She felt breathless and excited and couldn't believe this was happening to her.

The restaurant was tiny and exclusive and the food superb. Georgina ate everything that was placed in front of her and Leon watched with amused interest. 'It's nice to find a girl who doesn't push the food around her plate because she's watching her figure.'

'I never put on weight,' Georgina confided happily. 'I have a high metabolic rate, you see. I'm always full of pent-up energy. I work hard and play hard.'

A brow rose and he put down his knife and fork, seeming genuinely interested. 'You're a fitness freak?'

Georgina grinned. 'Not exactly, but I like swimming and badminton, and I do a fair amount of jogging. Any sort of sport, really.'

'Do you play tennis?'

She nodded.

'Then you'll have to give me a game some time.'

The thought that he wanted to see her again sent a thrill riding through her, though she was careful not to appear too enthusiastic. 'I'd like that.'

They lingered at the table long after they had finished eating, Leon smoking a cheroot, watching her lazily through the thin haze of smoke, making no secret of his interest in her.

She drank her coffee and the cup was refilled by an attentive waiter, and Leon encouraged her to talk about herself. 'Are you an only child?'

She laughed. 'Far from it. I have three brothers, all older than me, and when we were kids I always tried to keep up with them. I was a proper tomboy.'

'It doesn't show,' he grinned.

'And for as far back as I can remember I always wanted to be a garage mechanic when I grew up.'

He laughed. 'Do you know something, Georgina? I can see you doing that.'

'In this?' she asked mischievously, looking down at her ultra-feminine dress.

'I bet you look just as good in a pair of overalls.'

'I didn't become a mechanic,' she admitted. 'My parents were against it. I went to art college instead.'

His thick brows rose and she guessed he was thinking it was a far cry from messing about with engines.

'I took a course in textile design and finally got a job with a firm of design consultants.'

'Doing what?'

'Designing carpets, fabrics, tiles, and whatever. I didn't stay there, though. I wasn't happy, I wasn't active enough. Now I work for an interior design firm and I get out quite a lot. I love it.'

'So that cosy little flat you have was designed by your own fair hands?'

Georgina nodded. 'But that was in the early days. I'd make certain changes now, except that I'm hoping to buy somewhere of my own before too long so it's not really worth it.'

It was almost midnight when he suggested taking her home. 'I don't want my princess turning into a pumpkin.'

His princess! Georgina hid her delight. The evening had been far more successful than she could ever have imagined. She had accompanied Helen more out of curiosity than anything else, wanting to see the new owner of Puter Software, the man who, according to her friend, was making everyone's life a misery with his domineering ways.

And now she was here with him and he wasn't like that at all. He was human and kind, and warm and considerate, and his manner was too genuine to be a front.

He brought the car to a halt outside her flat and Georgina turned to him eagerly. 'Would you like to come up for some coffee? I've had a wonderful time, I don't really want the night to end.' The words were out before she could stop them.

'I'd love to, Georgina.' His tone was regretful and he seemed not to mind her enthusiasm. 'But I'm going to Scotland for the weekend and need to make an early start. I would like to see you again, though, when I come back.'

'I'd like that too,' she whispered.

He leaned across the space that separated them and the kiss he gave her was brief, his lips merely brushing hers, exciting her, thrilling her, but disappointing her also because she wanted more. Strong feelings had built up inside her during this remarkable evening and she wanted to feel his arms about her, wanted a proper kiss, wanted to savour to the full his sexuality. Even so she admired his restraint.

'Where did you get to last night?' Helen sat in Georgina's living-room, her eyes sulky and accusing.

Georgina smiled. 'Leon took me out to dinner.'

'He did what?' gasped her friend. 'Heavens, Georgina, you stupid girl. Haven't you ever listened to anything I've told you about him?'

'I think you're biased,' said Georgina with a shrug. 'I found him most pleasant.'

'Oh, he would be, to start with. But I bet it didn't take him long to invite you into bed.'

'Helen!' Georgina's tone was shocked. 'How can you say that?'

'Because that's what he's like.'

'You don't know for sure; you're making it up because he didn't want to take you out. Please don't be jealous, Helen. I want you to be pleased for me.'

'So what happened?'

'What do you mean, what happened?'

'How far did he go?'

Georgina grimaced. 'He didn't try anything, Helen. He hardly even kissed me. It was a just a goodbye peck, that's all.'

'Do you expect me to believe that?'

'It's the truth.' Georgina's chin was high, her eyes hurt. 'He's not at all as you said he was. He's fantasic, and he's asked if he can see me again.'

'How about Craig? Are you going to tell him about Leon?'

'Craig doesn't own me,' retorted Georgina sharply.

'You've been going out with him for a long time,' reminded her friend.

'Nine months off and on—more off than on. He knows I don't love him. I wish he hadn't bought me that expensive gold necklace for Christmas and that bracelet for my birthday. It's most embarrassing.'

'And the flowers and the chocolates and the meals out,' pressed Helen. 'He must have a good job, that's all I can say.'

'He works for his uncle,' informed Georgina, 'who pays him a fantastic wage, so he says. His parents were killed when he was ten so he lives with his uncle and doesn't have to pay a penny for his upkeep. The man sounds crazy to me; he's certainly doing Craig no favours. I've never actually met his uncle, you understand. Craig's only ever taken me home when he's out.'

Craig was fun and they had some good times together, but she did not want to spend the rest of her life with him. He was a couple of years younger than herself although it wasn't obvious. He was tall and good-looking and he vowed he loved her, though she wasn't entirely sure that she believed him. And compared to Leon he was nothing but a boy!

She waited eagerly for Leon to ring, disappointed when several days went by and she heard nothing. Perhaps he was still in Scotland? Perhaps he was too busy? She refused to accept that he was not a man of his word.

Then her eldest brother, Ross, rang to say he was in town and needed company over a meal. It was Saturday night and she was supposed to be meeting Craig but he wasn't too put out when she told him. 'So long as he is your brother,' he warned.

'He really is,' she insisted.

'I've actually heard all about him,' he admitted. 'He's made quite a name for himself in the computer trade.'

'His company is now one of the biggest,' admitted Georgina. 'I'm very proud of him.' And funnily enough one of his main competitors was Puter Software!

Puter Software wasn't Leon's only business interest, she had discovered. He had his finger in many pies, but this was his latest acquisition and he was spending all his time there. It was said that he intended making it the biggest and best computer software company in the British Isles, probably in the world.

Georgina hadn't seen Ross since Christmas and her welcome was enthusiastic. 'You look good, Ross, I do miss you. How's Mary? And my nephews? Still driving you crazy?'

He groaned. 'Don't mention it. I know now how our parents felt when we were young. I don't mind telling you, Gina, I'm glad to get out of the house sometimes.'

Georgina grinned. Her nephews were terrors, aged three and five and as full of life as Ross and her other brothers had been at the same age. 'You'll survive. Where are you taking me?'

'Jerome's. Nothing but the best for my little sister.'

Jerome's! Where Leon had taken her! They obviously had similar tastes in other things besides business.

The restaurant was busy, their table in one corner, and Georgina had her back to the room. It was not until they got up to leave that she saw Leon Alexander. And he wasn't alone! A very pretty blonde was giving him her full attention.

His eyes narrowed when he saw her with Ross, flickering from one to the other, acknowledging her brother gravely, his eyes enigmatic when they switched to her.

Georgina felt an arrow of jealousy stab her. It looked as though Helen was right after all in saying that he wasn't content with one girl. If he dared to ring her now she would tell him exactly what to do with himself.

But he did not ring and as days turned into weeks she made herself forget him. She continued to see Craig occasionally, and he continued to tell her that he loved her, but she suspected he might be dating someone else and she was pleased for him. Perhaps he had at last got the message.

Then late one Saturday night Craig phoned her. 'I'm leaving the country,' he said without preamble, sounding as though he was having difficulty in keeping his voice steady.

'Craig, what do you mean? Where are you going? Why? Isn't this rather sudden?'

'I've been offered a job in Texas that's too good to resist. I'm leaving tomorrow.'

'Tomorrow?' Georgina was flabbergasted. 'What sort of a job? You've never said anything about it.'

'I suppose it's been on the cards for a long time—but it's only just happened. I'm sorry, Gina. I'm going to miss you.'

'Craig, I don't understand. I'm coming to see you.'

'No, don't!' He sounded panic-stricken. 'It's for the best. I've accepted the fact that you'll never love me.'

'So it's my fault, is it?' Georgina swallowed a sudden lump in her throat. 'You're doing this because of—us?'

'You could say that. I must go, Gina, I have my packing to do. I'll never forget you. Thanks for the good times we've had together.'

Georgina stood for a long time after she had put down the phone. Something didn't add up. He would have told her, surely, if he had been planning something like this? To just spring it on her wasn't in Craig's nature. And if she had loved him, really loved him, then she would have been round there now finding out exactly what was going on. But since she didn't love him, and since he had made a point of mentioning it, then it would be wisest to let him go. It still didn't make sense, though.

Several days went by and the mystery of Craig's departure still puzzled her. Then one evening she answered the intercom connected to the main door of the building and heard Leon Alexander's well-remembered growl.

Craig was instantly forgotten. Her heart hammered violently within her breast. After all this time he had come to see her! What should she do? Let him in or tell him to go away? His voice sounded impatient. 'Georgina, I want to see you—*now!*'

It wasn't the sexual growl she remembered so well. It was a command, and instinctively she moved to obey, pressing the switch which released the lock. She heard his tread on the stairs, taking them two or three at a time, suggesting that whatever he wanted to see her about was urgent.

She had the door open and waiting, a tentative smile on her lips, but it changed to an inward shiver when she saw the dark hardness of his face. This wasn't a friendly visit, that was for sure. He was angry, deeply angry, his jaw taut, his grey eyes dark and condemning. What on earth had she done to deserve this?

Georgina lifted her chin and stepped back for him to enter, catching a whiff of his distinctive aftershave as he brushed past her. She closed the door and followed him into her living-room.

He turned and looked at her, and although it was her own flat Georgina knew what it was like to beard a lion in its den. 'What's this all about?' she asked.

'You should know.'

'Should I?' Her expression was bewildered. He was making no sense, none at all.

He walked towards her and hooked his fingers beneath the thin gold chain she wore. 'Did Craig buy you this?'

'Yes, but——'

Without further ado, and before she could stop him, he yanked it from her throat. 'And this bracelet?'

'Yes.'

That too was torn from her wrist and Georgina was too stunned to do anything about it.

'How many more litle trinkets has Craig bought you?' he sneered.

She rubbed her neck and wrist and glared at him furiously. 'How do you know about Craig? What's going on?'

'Craig is my nephew,' he snorted, 'as if you didn't know.'

'Of course I didn't know,' she choked, unable to believe that she was hearing him correctly. It was too much of a coincidence. He was Craig's uncle? She could not believe it.

'Didn't you ever stop to wonder where Craig got all his money from?'

'He told me he worked for his uncle—you, it would appear—and that he earned a good wage and you didn't want anything for his upkeep. It sounded logical although I did try to stop him spending his money on me.'

'You didn't try very hard,' he growled. 'If at all. You're nothing more than a fortune hunter, a tramp, a disgusting little gold-digger.'

Georgina gasped. 'How dare you?' She was seeing now the side of him that Helen had told her about. There was no comparison with the warm, caring man she had met at the cocktail party. None at all. He was hard and distant and distinctly obnoxious.

'Oh, I dare,' he told her coldly. 'And I suggest you don't look so outraged. You really can't have thought you'd get away with it.'

'Away with what?' she choked. He was talking in riddles. He was making no sense at all.

'Trying to get as much out of Craig as you could, to the extent that he had to steal from me to keep you happy.'

'What?' Georgina frowned in confusion. What was the man talking about? 'Craig told you that?'

'When I confronted him with defrauding Tentronics— another one of my companies, as you must know—he told me he had a girlfriend with expensive tastes. Oh, he was clever, believe me. I wouldn't have found out if he hadn't made a stupid mistake.'

'Defrauding?' Georgina's tone was quiet now. It was all too much to take in. 'Why would he do that? I never asked him for anything. I didn't want any of his presents. He insisted. I——'

'Don't give me that rubbish,' he snarled. 'It would have been a simple matter to refuse. The truth of the matter is that you knew when you were on to a good thing.'

'I want to speak to Craig,' she said firmly, her eyes now as cold as his. She did not believe that he had gone abroad. Leon had simply forbidden him to see her again.

'He's in Texas,' he informed her coolly. 'I should have called in the police, but that would have meant involving you—and I intend dealing with you myself.'

The look he gave her was full of stone-cold hatred. No one had ever looked at her like that before, it was a totally new experience. Her spine stiffened and fingers of ice reached out inside to chill each one of her limbs.

'Instead he's working for my brother,' he went on relentlessly. 'Harry won't stand any nonsense. If Craig puts one foot wrong he'll wish he were dead.'

Georgina sank down into a chair. It was all too much to take in. Every vestige of colour drained from her face and she felt physically sick. Leon Alexander was fully convinced that she was involved and she knew that whatever she said, no matter how strongly she tried to defend herself, he wouldn't believe her. It was there in his eyes, he was totally condemning. How a man could change so much she did not know.

'And I suppose you thought you'd get even more out of me?'

Her head jerked, her eyes flashing green. 'What the hell's that supposed to mean?'

'Oh, come on, Georgina. It was no coincidence that we met on the night of the cocktail party. You had it planned, didn't you? I saw you watching me right from the moment you entered the room. I should have known then that you were another of those predatory females who make my life hell.'

Georgina jumped to her feet. 'How dare you? I came because Helen asked me, certainly not to meet someone as obnoxious as you.'

'You didn't seem to find me obnoxious when I took you out to dinner. If I remember rightly you invited me back for coffee. Were you also planning to ask me to stay the night?'

'Your mind's a sewer,' she spat. 'I had no ulterior motive whatsoever. I really enjoyed your company, and that is all. And I know nothing about what you're accusing Craig of doing.'

He snorted angry disbelief. 'Quite an actress. But you don't convince me, not for one minute. And you'll live to regret it, Georgina, believe me. You're going to wish you'd never heard the name Leon Alexander.'

CHAPTER TWO

'GINA, I have some good news for you.'

Georgina smiled at her employer as she walked into her office. She could certainly do with something to cheer her up after the bombshell Leon had dropped a few days earlier. She was still trying to pick up the pieces.

She found it totally incredible that Craig should have stolen from his uncle's company simply to give her a good time. She'd had no idea, not the slightest inkling that he was doing anything like that. She would have stopped him straight away, and now she had spent sleepless nights worrying and wondering what Leon Alexander was going to do about it.

'I've had this marvellous enquiry,' went on Valerie Arden. 'Well, more than an enquiry actually. It's a definite assignment, and the client has asked for you.'

Georgina felt pleased. It meant she was beginning to earn a reputation in her own right as an interior designer. More and more often these days people asked for her by name.

'It might mean you spending some time away from home,' went on her glamorous boss. Valerie Arden was tall and energetic and wore fashionable clothes which she gave her own individual look with dramatic accessories. 'That won't be any problem, will it?'

'Of course not,' answered Georgina at once. It wouldn't be the first time she had had to do it, and a change of scenery was just what she wanted. Anything to take her mind off the unfortunate sequence of events that had led to Leon Alexander's accusation. 'Where exactly will I be going?'

'Scotland.'

'Scotland?' She hadn't realised that her reputation had travelled so far.

'Yes, the client wishes to convert a Victorian country mansion into a hotel. It might mean your being away for several weeks, months perhaps.'

'That's all right—it sounds exciting,' smiled Georgina. In fact it was perfect. 'Who recommended me?'

'I'm not sure. But the client's name is...' Valerie consulted the sheet of paper in her hand. 'Alexander. Leon Alexander. I've never heard of him before, but he's obviously heard about us.'

Georgina felt the blood drain out of her face and she went deathly cold. Valerie looked at her with a frown. 'Is something wrong? Don't you feel well?'

Georgina swallowed hard. 'It's nothing. I just—can't someone else do it?'

'Gina? What is it?'

With an effort she pulled herself together. This was nonsense. It was coincidence. It had nothing whatsoever to do with Craig—or Leon's threat! 'I was surprised, that's all. I know Leon—at least we've met.'

'There you are, then,' said Valerie with a relieved smile. 'That's why he's asked for you. You must have made quite an impression.'

Georgina grimaced and nodded. 'I suppose I did.' But not in the way Valerie was thinking! 'I can't go, Valerie. We—we didn't hit it off. I can't work for that man, I really can't.' It would be an impossible situation. She hadn't taken his threat seriously but now she knew that he had meant every word. Somehow, some way, he was going to make her pay for what he thought she had done.

Valerie's frown returned, grooving her normally smooth brow. 'What nonsense. This is business. You can't let your private life interfere.'

Georgina swallowed hard and looked down at her feet. 'I'm sorry, Valerie, I really can't do it.'

'Mr Alexander asked for you specifically.' Valerie tutted her impatience. 'I can't afford to upset him, or, even worse, lose his business altogether—which he threatened me with if I didn't send you. Financially I'm going through a bad patch, Gina. You obviously don't realise that, but I need this order. It's a big commission and could lead to further useful business. I'm afraid I'll have to insist.'

Still Georgina hesitated. Valerie had no idea what she was asking her to do.

'Well, Georgina?' Valerie was clearly losing her patience.

'Please, can't you send someone else?' she pleaded. 'How about Melanie? She's as good as me. I'm sure——'

'No, I cannot.' Valerie's grim tone suggested that Georgina either accept or find herself out of a job.

Perhaps it wouldn't be for long, she thought unhappily. Certainly not the months her employer had spoken of. Please not months. She couldn't spend that much time with him. Or was she worrying for nothing? He wouldn't be there, would he, after he had given her her brief? He had other much more important things to do. She smiled faintly. 'OK, I'll go.'

Relief filled Valerie Arden's eyes. 'Good girl, I knew you'd see sense. Whatever it is that's happened between you two, just push it to the back of your mind. Now, let's see.' She looked again at the piece of paper. 'He's very anxious to get things started straight away. He says that the structural alterations are almost complete. Could you go up to Scotland the day after tomorrow?'

No respite! Georgina swallowed nervously and her stomach churned like a food mixer. 'Yes, I expect so.'

'You've no commitments you can't get out of?'

'No.'

Valerie looked pleased. 'That's settled, then. Mr Alexander has arranged for you to fly up there, but I'll give you all the details tomorrow. I almost wish I were going myself. It will be one of the largest projects you've ever done. Make a good job of this, Gina, and you'll make your name. But I don't have to tell you that, do I?'

On Wednesday a chauffeur-driven Mercedes turned up outside Georgina's flat with Leon inside. And he definitely had not got over his anger. His face was taut, his tanned skin stretched tightly across prominent cheekbones, his lips clamped, hiding the whiteness of his teeth.

But Georgina was determined not to let him see that he intimidated her and she smiled brilliantly as she climbed in beside him. 'Thank you very much for asking me to do this job. It's a wonderful opportunity. I'm really looking forward to it.'

For just an instant she saw the stunned look on his face. He clearly had not expected her to be so cheerful. Then it was gone. 'You needn't look so pleased; you're going to have to work hard, damned hard.'

'I didn't doubt it for one second,' she replied easily, still smiling. 'I don't mind hard work. In fact I thrive on it.'

His nostrils flared and his eyes grew glacial; Georgina's lips quirked as she had a sudden vision of him breathing out fire. He was so angry she could imagine him igniting inside.

'What's so damn funny?' he snarled.

'You are,' she said, looking him straight in the eye. Her mother had always said that the best antidote to crying was laughter, and so whenever Georgina was upset she hid it behind a veneer of amusement. Many times she had laughed while tears coursed down her cheeks, but it had worked—and she rarely got angry these days. 'It's unbelievable that you're still blaming me for what Craig did.'

'I have no reason not to.'

'You have my word.'

'Which means nothing.'

'I am not in the habit of lying, Mr Alexander.'

'And I, Miss Gregory, am a pretty shrewd judge of character, quite apart from the fact that I have proof of the type of woman you are.'

A quick frown furrowed Georgina's brow. 'Proof? What proof? What are you talking about?'

'I think you know, but as you prefer to play dumb then I will tell you.'

He paused, ensuring he had her full attention, and Georgina felt her heart rate quicken until it sounded like a drumbeat in her ears.

At that moment his car phone rang and while he was talking, his voice reverting to its sensual growl, Georgina was able to study him.

He wore blue trousers this morning and a navy blazer, and a gold ring studded with a large diamond. On some men it would have been flashy but on Leon it was no such thing. He had large hands, well manicured, with soft dark hairs glinting at this moment in the sunlight slanting in through the car windows. His aftershave filled the car, not overpowering like the man himself, but subtle and tantalising, a clean, fresh smell.

His call finished, his eyes were on her again, and he spoke as though he had not been interrupted. 'Point one, you made sure I'd notice you at that party——'

'I did no such thing,' she cut in acidly, her fingers clenched tightly on her bag, her eyes shocked.

'And what galls most,' he went on, 'is that you almost fooled me, despite the fact that it's been tried on so often in the past that I ought to have known.'

'So it's yourself you're angry with?'

'Point two,' he said firmly, 'I saw you trying exactly the same thing with Ross Hanchurch.'

This time Georgina really did laugh, causing the chauffeur to look through his mirror to see what had caused the amusement. Though Georgina felt sure he was listening avidly to every word they said. 'Ross is my brother.'

'With a different surname?'

'OK, my half-brother.' She rarely remembered that Ross's father had died and his mother remarried before she was born.

'What a fertile imagination you have, Miss Gregory. I suppose you're going to tell me next that it wasn't your fault my nephew was besotted with you?'

'No, it wasn't,' she said at once. 'I didn't ask for his love, I didn't love him, I——'

'Don't go any further. I know exactly what your plans were. But what is it they say, "much wants more and greedy wants the lot"? You weren't satisfied with Craig's paltry little gifts, were you, you——'

'Paltry?' echoed Georgina disbelievingly. 'They——'

'You set your sights a little higher,' he carried on as though she had not spoken. 'But it didn't work. I've had my fill of engineering females. If anyone does the chasing it's me. I think you should be made to suffer for what you've done.'

Again his phone went and again Georgina sat and waited, amazed that he could shut himself off from one conversation and use an entirely different tone of voice.

'Designing the interior of a hotel won't be hard work, Mr Alexander. It's a job I'll enjoy,' she said when he had finished.

For the first time he smiled, but it held no pleasure. 'I shall personally make sure that you derive no gratification from it. You'll work hard and long hours in a remote area which is far removed from anything you're used to.'

Georgina refused to let him antagonise her further. Deliberately she turned her attention to the passing scenery.

'I've got through to you, have I?'

His harsh tone made Georgina jerk back towards him. 'Lack of people or conveniences doesn't worry me, Mr Alexander. I shall do my job to the best of my ability and that's all there is to it.'

He nodded. 'You have spirit, I'll admit that.'

'I've always had to fight my own battles,' she told him shortly, and at that moment the car stopped.

Georgina had not been looking where they were going and was surprised to see a small private airport. 'Where are we?'

'It's not important,' he said brusquely.

His chauffeur opened their doors and Leon led her, his hand on her elbow as though he were afraid she might try to run away, to a waiting twin-engined Cessna. Despite the alarm she felt at the situation in which she now found herself, Georgina could not ignore the warmth that ran through her at his touch, the very real awareness of Leon as a sexual male animal. She doubted, whatever the situation between them, that these feelings would go away. He had made too deep an impression on her in the very first place.

'Is this your private plane?' she asked as they climbed the steps up to the cabin, the chauffeur following with their luggage.

'That's right.' Leon's lips curled back, revealing his large, even teeth. 'But surely you knew that? You're aware that I'm a very wealthy man; that's the reason you found me so attractive, isn't it?'

'I know you're the most infuriating man I've ever met,' she retorted, sitting down in the first seat she came to. 'Money doesn't enter into it. I've done none of the things you accuse me of, and yet you're intent on whisking me away to some remote little spot in order to give me a hard time. Why?'

He sat beside her, ignoring the other seats which would have given her breathing space. 'Oh, come on, Georgina, you know why.' As he spoke his eyes fell on the gold chain around her neck. 'Is that another one of Craig's baubles?'

His hand moved towards her and she jerked backwards. 'You leave that alone. My parents gave it to me when I was twenty-one.'

A mocking brow rose. 'Is that so? You look no more than eighteen. Fasten your seatbelt.'

She obeyed and almost immediately the plane raced along the runway. Georgina instinctively held on to the arms of her seat.

'Don't you like flying?' he frowned.

'Would it matter if I said no?'

'Not really, at least not at this stage. I imagine you'd have said if you had any real fear.'

'I've been given no chance to say anything,' she said accusingly. 'I tried to get out of this job but Valerie insisted. You really did a good job on her, didn't you?'

'I did my homework,' he admitted with a satisfied smile. 'I discovered she was in financial difficulties. The rest was easy. How old are you?'

'Twenty-five.'

'And not married? Why is that? Haven't you yet found anyone rich enough?' he goaded.

Georgina refused to answer. Arguing with this man got her nowhere; it was wiser to remain silent.

'What was Craig?' he demanded. 'A fill-in until someone better came along?'

Stung into retaliation, Georgina flashed, 'I never encouraged Craig.' They were airborne and she looked out of the window, watching the chequered patchwork of fields grow more and more distant, disappearing altogether when they flew above the clouds into a world of sunlight. Here was the cloudscape, the marvellous formations that looked like fallen snow.

'You didn't actively discourage him, either. No man would shower a woman with gifts unless he felt he was getting somewhere, especially someone as young and impressionable as my nephew.'

'I told him I didn't love him.'

'But you didn't tell him to keep away? You still accepted his presents.' His cold grey eyes whiplashed her. 'You must have thought you were on to a good thing.'

'You're detestable.'

'And you're a shameless, money-grabbing hypocrite.'

'How dare you?' Georgina raised her hand to strike him, anger for once getting the better of her, but he caught her wrist easily.

'I promise you, Georgina, that if you hit me I won't think twice about hitting you back.'

'Only a coward would hit a woman.'

'Or a man who's been pushed to his limits.'

'You don't have to accompany me,' she jerked, wondering what he meant by that remark. 'In fact you didn't have to force me into this job. I don't know why you did, I don't know what pleasure you're going to get out of it.'

'I think I'll get a lot of pleasure,' he said.

'You're after your pound of flesh, is that it? I'm supposed to make up for whatever it is you claim Craig has stolen?'

'Something like that,' he admitted easily.

She shook her head. 'I can't believe this. He didn't spend enough on me to have to steal. Unless you weren't paying him a decent wage after all. Is that it?'

'He didn't spend enough?' he ejaculated incredulously. 'You don't call thousands of pounds enough? My God, what sort of a female are you?'

'*Thousands?*' echoed Georgina disbelievingly. 'What are you talking about?'

'You're very good at acting the innocent, aren't you?' he sneered.

'Because I am innocent,' she protested strongly.

'Are you trying to tell me that he spent the money on other things, other women perhaps?'

'No, I am not,' she exploded. 'I actually don't think for one minute that he took it, and I don't have to take this from you.' It was getting more and more difficult to hold her temper. He was the most infuriating man she had ever met. Helen was right. He was unbearable.

'You have no choice, my dear.'

Georgina glared. 'Everyone has a free choice. When I get off this plane I'm turning right round and going home, and if I lose my job it will be preferable to working for a monster like you.'

He seemed to find her ill-temper amusing; he was actually smiling now, relaxing back in his seat and watching her as one might a child. 'You're here to do a job, Georgina, and that job you're going to do, even if I have to keep you prisoner.'

'How about your other business interests?' she sneered, refusing to let him intimidate her. 'Especially the new software company that you're busy turning into a multi-million-pound concern?'

'It can manage without me,' he answered easily. 'Although I have in fact set up an office in Scotland so that I can keep my finger on every pulse.'

Georgina shook her head. It was difficult to keep up with this man.

'You don't believe me?'

'Oh, I believe you all right. In future I'll believe everything I'm told about you. Do you know what I think, Mr Alexander? I don't think it's so much what Craig has done, I think you enjoy using your power over women. I think that's it. According to what I've heard there have been a lot of women in your life, and somewhere along the line you had a bad experience. It made you bitter, did it? You enjoy taking the whip out and cutting us down to size. Is that what this is all about?'

Georgina had never spoken to anyone like this before, but then again she had never met anyone like Leon Alexander. It looked as though she would have to put up with him for the next few weeks—he was not going to let her get away easily—but how she was going to do it she did not know. It was going to be the worst assignment of her career. If only she hadn't gone to that party; if only she had never met him.

'If you know what's good for you you'll keep your mouth shut about my past,' he snarled, his eyes narrowing to mere slits, and Georgina could almost feel the anger vibrating from him. It was obvious that she had come very close to the truth.

She glanced out of the window at the mounds of white cloud. A long silence fell between them. Somewhere beneath was the countryside of England and Scotland. They had probably crossed the border by now.

She turned back again to Leon. 'Where exactly are we going?'

'A little place called Stramore in Wester Ross.' He had controlled his anger and now smiled at her, though there was still a tautness to his features that suggested it still simmered below the surface. 'We shouldn't be much longer.'

'I've never heard of it.'

'Not many people have. It's as I said, very remote. I'll be offering a perfect, get-away-from-it-all holiday. The mansion stands in roughly a hundred and twenty acres of woodland and lawns. There'll be horse riding, fishing, golf, a tennis court for the more energetic, a heated swimming pool, and many more activities. Our guests will be able to do nothing or everything, depending on what mood they're in. And if they don't want to drive we'll provide chauffeur-driven cars to take them on sight-seeing tours, mini-buses for larger groups. Expensive but luxurious, that's my aim.'

Georgina was impressed—and excited too. It would be the biggest challenge of her career. Little did Leon Alexander know it, but he was doing her a favour. 'So there'll be no expense spared as far as the interior's concerned?'

'None at all. I'll brief you when we get there.' Even as he spoke the plane lost height. For a moment Georgina saw nothing but swirling white cloud, then came the thrilling, majestic sweep of mountains, some with tiny pockets of snow in shady places, and the occasional glint of water.

They landed on a tiny airstrip a few miles north of the Kyle of Lochalsh where a car was waiting for them. Leon never left her side for one second, making sure she did not have the chance to run away, throwing their luggage into the boot and taking the wheel. For the first few miles he drove in silence. The road was narrow, flanked on either side by huge masses of rhododendrons, past their best now but impressive nevertheless.

'Loch Carron,' he said shortly as the road began to climb, 'and the world-famous Kyle railway line.' Georgina looked down at the long tongue of water below and the track running parallel with the road. But as the road twisted and turned and climbed and fell, picking its way through a pine forest, she caught no more than tantalising glimpses of the loch.

The road took them round to the other side of the loch, through the town of Lochcarron which hugged the lochside, on through the mountains where they had to continually stop to let sheep get out of their way. 'They have absolutely no road sense,' Leon informed her, 'and are totally oblivious to car horns and lights. All we can do is wait.'

Georgina forgot her antagonism in her enthusiasm for the beauty of the Highlands. 'I don't care, I just love it here. I've never been to Scotland before. It's magnificent.'

He nodded curtly. 'You'd best make the most of it, because you'll have no time for sightseeing once we're there.'

They came to Loch Kishorn and then headed directly north through miles of rugged mountains and very little else.

Georgina's enthusiasm was not dampened by Leon's brusque remarks. 'However did you find this place?' It seemed to her that they were in the middle of nowhere—and would anyone really want to holiday here?

He shrugged. 'I have contacts. I've been looking for somewhere in this region for a long time.' He turned off the main road, climbing through the forest, and suddenly they were high up above another loch, a beautiful loch with tiny green islands and green, blue and grey waters.

Georgina was so busy looking down that she was unprepared when the car stopped. They had entered a clearing and now before them stood the house.

'Stramore House,' he announced proudly.

Georgina looked at the grey stone mansion with its rounded turrets at one end that made it look as though it had once been a castle. Ivy climbed its walls and it was larger than she had expected. Excitement coursed through her. There were workmen's cars and trucks parked in front, and the sound of hammering and sawing and cheerful whistling came from within.

'We'll take a quick look around and then I'll show you where you're staying. I've no doubt you'll want to freshen up and have something to eat.'

Georgina wasn't listening; she was already running up the steps to the house. A scene of chaos met her eyes. Leon had said that the structural alterations were almost complete. It must have been wishful thinking.

He followed and she heard the sudden roar of his voice. *'Angus!'*

The whole house went silent, then footsteps sounded on the stairs.

'Angus, what the hell's going on?' asked Leon before the man was even in sight. 'I thought you told me everything would be finished this weekend? It doesn't look that way to me.'

Angus was small and thin and wiry, with keen blue eyes and a sunburned face. 'Och, well, we had a wee problem, but it's nothing at all to worry about.'

'I am worried, Angus,' insisted Leon. 'What problem? Why wasn't I told?'

The man lifted his bony shoulders. 'There was a delay in some of the materials. It couldn't be helped. They've arrived now.'

'How far behind are we?' Leon's tone was quiet but Georgina was beginning to realise that this was when he was at his most dangerous.

'A couple more weeks should see most of the work done.'

'See to it that it's no longer,' said Leon tightly. 'Work overtime if necessary. This is Georgina Gregory, who's looking after the interior decorations. Georgina, Angus Gillies.'

Angus wiped his hand on the seat of his pants. 'Pleased to meet you, lassie. If you were thinking of having a look around I'd better warn the men to mind their language.'

Georgina grinned. 'It doesn't matter. I don't shock easily.' She felt sorry for the little man.

But all whistling and talking stopped as they picked their way through piles of debris and Georgina was aware of their eyes on her. In her high heels and cream suit she must have looked completely out of place.

Leon accompanied her, pointing out what was going to be the restaurant with its impressive vaulted ceiling, two conference rooms, and a large lounge. Upstairs they looked at a couple of the bedrooms and one of the suites.

'I'm leaving everything to you,' he said. 'You can see what the house is like and I want it in keeping. I want it luxurious but I don't want you to go overboard. Comfort is of prime importance, however. I want the guests to feel as comfortable as if they were in their own home.'

She nodded and could not contain her enthusiasm. 'This is fantastic. I can already picture some of the rooms in my mind.'

'Naturally I wish to approve your designs before you go ahead.' He shared none of her passion for the project. 'And I'm warning you now that I'm a hard man to please. We'll go now, and you can come tomorrow and spend as much time here as you like.'

Georgina nodded happily. 'I'm really going to love this.' There was no answering pleasure on his face but she refused to let him dampen her spirits. 'I've never been let loose on a project this size.'

'You are capable?' A frown sliced through the granite hardness of his brow. 'I'm not going to make an expensive mistake?'

'I imagine you had me checked out before you approached my employer,' she answered calmly, 'just as you did Valerie's company. You're a thorough man, I'm beginning to realise that, but if you think being stuck up here is going to be a penance, then you're mistaken. Hard work doesn't frighten me, Mr Alexander. It won't worry me one little bit if I have no spare time to go out and enjoy myself. On the contrary, the harder I work the quicker the job will be finished, and that will suit me just fine.'

His lips tightened as he led the way back out to his car and they followed the road higher up the mountain. It narrowed until it became nothing more than a track, and finally they came to a halt outside a tiny cottage. There were no other houses.

They got out of the car and Georgina looked at him questioningly. 'We're staying here?' The two of them! *Together!* This was something she hadn't counted on.

'Just you.'

'Me! By myself! But why? Where are you going?'

A hint of a smile appeared. 'Are you suggesting you would like me to join you?'

'No!' Her denial was loud and emphatic, though her heart clamoured at the thought. There had been a time, a very brief time, when she would have welcomed such a proposal. 'I'm suggesting that neither of us stay here. It's totally unsuitable.'

'On the contrary, I think it will be eminently suitable. When Stramore House was first built this was the gardener's cottage. Down the years one of the sons fancied himself as an artist and a studio was put on at the back. I thought it would be a perfect place for you to work.'

She glanced at him scornfully. 'How thoughtful. Where are you staying?' The fact was she did not mind being on her own, but he could not have known that. This was probably a part of his devious plan to make her suffer.

'I have a room at the inn in Stramore itself.'

'Why can't I stay there too?'

'Because you're out of Craig's way here,' he said grimly.

Her eyes widened in disbelief. 'Craig's in Texas—or so you said!'

'He's also quite likely to run away if the going gets too hard,' he scorned. 'And I don't want him to be able to get in touch with you.'

'You're a swine!' she spat. 'I can't really see it stopping him finding me if he really wanted to.'

'There is another reason.'

She lifted her brows and waited for him to tell her.

'You're a very beautiful girl, Georgina. At the inn other men would make passes at you, and I don't want that to happen.'

'Other men?' she queried, her face contorted with disbelief. 'I'm not interested in other men, for heaven's sake.'

'Not unless they have plenty of money?'

Georgina let her breath out in a hiss and felt like scratching his eyes out. 'I told you before you have a mind like a sewer. It stinks. Was it a woman who did this to you, or have you always been distrustful of the female sex?'

His eyes narrowed until she could no longer see them. 'That's enough, Georgina.'

She shrugged. 'OK, if you don't want to talk about it. It seems to me, though, that whatever it is it's festering inside you and you need help.'

'Not from you,' he snarled.

'So I'm stuck with this cottage?' She decided a change of subject was advisable. 'Tell me, is there water here or do I have to bathe in a mountain spring?'

'What a tantalising thought that conjures up.' The tension had gone.

Georgina grew warm as he looked at her and for a second there was a sensual gleam in his eyes. It was one of his rare flashes as a red-blooded male and it reminded her of their first meeting. Her heart raced unchecked for a moment. He had shown a definite interest in her then. Would those moments ever be recaptured?

'There's running water and also a generator,' he told her at length. 'I'll show you how it works.' He strode ahead with her cases and Georgina picked up a holdall and followed. He had a long, easy stride, his whole body relaxed, and yet his face, when she caught him up at the door, was set into its already familiar taut lines.

It was dark and cool inside the cottage, both the thick walls and the trees surrounding it keeping out the warmth of the sun. She shivered. It had a distinctly unwelcoming feel.

She wasn't afraid, nothing like that, but some places felt comfortable and some didn't, and this was one of those that didn't. She shivered as she stood in the centre of the room and looked around her. There were handmade rag rugs on the stone floor and a pair of easy chairs flanked the fireplace. There was a table and chairs and it was reasonably clean. She supposed she could be thankful it wasn't any worse. A few personal touches would make all the difference. Pictures and flowers and perhaps some brassware.

'The kitchen's through here,' he announced. 'I left instructions for it to be stocked with food. Ah, yes.' He looked into the larder and refrigerator and nodded. 'And this is the studio.'

It was a surprisingly large room at the back of the cottage with a sloping glass roof which let in the filtered sunlight. It was ten degrees warmer than the rest of the house.

'Yes, this is good, I can work in here,' she smiled. 'I need somewhere with good, clear daylight when I'm selecting colours.' There was a desk of sorts and cupboards. 'I presume if I need anything else you can get it for me?'

He nodded. 'Of course.'

Outside in a lean-to shed was the generator. 'This is the start switch,' he demonstrated. 'It's on now, of course, because of the refrigerator. It also runs your lights and the cooking stove. It's petrol-driven and I'm assured there's a full tank so you should have no problem.' Georgina had expected it to be very loud but in fact it ran quite silently. She was impressed.

Back indoors he took her cases upstairs, Georgina following. The bedroom was small but adequate and the bed looked as though it had been freshly made.

'Is this the bathroom?' She pushed open another door, but it was merely a box-room, stacked with what looked like canvases. Belonging to the erstwhile artist, she presumed.

'There is no bathroom,' Leon informed her. 'The toilet's downstairs and you'll have to wash at the kitchen sink. It's a bit primitive but I'm sure you'll survive.' He turned and left the room. 'I'll meet you at Stramore House at nine sharp in the morning.'

CHAPTER THREE

GEORGINA unpacked her clothes and put them away, and afterwards she cut some roses and put them in a bowl on the table. It instantly cheered the cottage up. She cooked herself a cheese omelette which she ate with sliced tomatoes and crusty bread, and followed it with a glass of milk. Afterwards she wandered outside, sitting down on an old wooden bench, mulling over the events that had led to her being here.

It had all happened so quickly. A few weeks ago she had not even met Leon Alexander. Now they were here, together, and he was doing his best to make her life a misery. She still found it difficult to accept that Craig had stolen from his uncle's firm, and to say that she had been involved was ridiculous. Yet Leon had it fixed firmly in his mind that she was interested in men only for the state of their bank balances—and how they got their money didn't matter.

The more Georgina thought about the situation, the more angry she became. Her fingers clutched the edge of the seat and she sat rigidly upright. She had been a fool to let Valerie persuade her. On the other hand she thought a lot of her employer. She hadn't been aware that the business was in difficulties until Valerie had mentioned it, and her conscience would have troubled her if she had dug in her heels and refused to do this job. She had really had no choice.

A movement in the trees caught her eye, and there, not twenty yards away, looking straight at her, stood a deer, and then came another, and another, until there was a whole family. Leon was forgotten—Georgina became entranced. She held her breath and watched, then unthinkingly lifted her arm. The sudden movement startled them and they turned and fled. She heard them darting through the undergrowth until all was silent again. Some of the tension had gone out of her.

A cuckoo called as it flew above the cottage, wrens warbled, and in the distance she heard the hammering of a woodpecker. Georgina had never been in a spot so closely linked to nature. There was something different up here—even the air was different—and she wished that the circumstances that had brought her here had been different also.

It was a strong place where the elements ruled. Now, in the middle of summer, it was peaceful, but she could imagine how stark and desolate it would be in the depths of winter. She shivered and thought of Leon again.

That night she surprised herself by sleeping easily and deeply, waking with a sense of excitement. Whatever happened, life wasn't going to be dull up here. She pulled on jeans and a light sweater, because even at this time of year the air felt cool and the sky was grey.

As she walked down to Stramore House she was dominated by the Scots pines, Britain's only large native conifer, rising tall and stately up to the very sky itself. There was no sign of the deer this morning, no sign of life at all except for the distant twittering of birds.

When the house came into sight Georgina saw Leon's car and she glanced at her watch. She did not want to be late and give him further cause for complaint. But it was only a quarter to nine. Even so, she hurried the last few yards.

She found him talking to Angus in the main entrance hall. Some of the debris had been cleared and she was able to walk without picking her way over rubble and planks.

'Good morning Mr Alexander, Angus,' she said brightly.

Angus smiled and returned her greeting, but Leon merely gave a curt nod and continued to talk.

Once they had finished, and the little man had gone, he turned to her. 'I trust you slept well?' His eyes were on her face, looking for tell-tale signs of a sleepless night.

'You hope no such thing,' she retorted smartly, 'but as a matter of fact, yes, I did, and I'm raring to start.'

Leon wore grey cotton trousers this morning and a short-sleeved white shirt, but the casual clothes made him no less imposing. 'You didn't mind being alone?' Still he was watching her and Georgina felt the full power of his sensuality. He didn't flaunt it, he never flaunted it, but it was a part of him that could not be ignored— at any time!

'Not in the least,' she smiled. 'Have I disappointed you? Were you hoping that I'd be scared out of my wits?' She did not wait for him to answer, but went on, 'As a matter of fact I saw some roe deer last night. Who knows what else I might see? It's a delightfully fascinating little place you've found me. Thank you.'

His mouth firmed, 'Let's go.'

Georgina hid a smile as she followed him into what was going to be the dining-room. He obviously did not like to think that she might be enjoying herself.

'I've seen a lot of hotels,' he told her, 'that don't live up to their external image. Stramore House is not going to be like that. It's a Victorian building so I want Victorian elegance, blended with modern comforts, of course. You are to choose everything from light-fittings to carpets, from furniture to the colour of the toilet rolls.

I don't want any of the rooms to be dark and stuffy, but not clinically white either. Do I make myself clear?'

'Perfectly,' she answered, 'and if you don't mind I prefer to look around by myself. I'll make notes and sketches which we can discuss later.'

Leon frowned. 'That could be a waste of time. I prefer to accompany you.'

'Maybe you will be useful,' she said absently, her mind already running on ahead. 'As some of the rooms aren't finished I need to know what they're going to be like. But perhaps someone else could help me? I'm sure you have work to do. Didn't you say something about setting up an office here?'

'I have a room at the inn, but I've also installed a very efficient secretary who will get in touch with me if I'm needed.'

In other words he intended sticking to her side like glue. Mental harassment! Georgina shrugged. Maybe he'd get fed up.

She went from room to room, studying, thinking, making detailed notes, saying nothing to Leon, and she could sense his growing anger.

'I'd like to know what you have in mind,' he said when they were standing in one of the bedrooms which had superb views over the loch and the whitewashed cottages hugging the far shoreline.

'What?' She turned to him absently. 'I'm sorry, I didn't hear what you said.'

'You've been ignoring me all morning,' he rasped.

'That's because I'm working. Isn't that what I'm supposed to be doing?'

'I think you should consult me.'

'You've already told me the image you wish to convey.'

'And how do I know that you will interpret it correctly?'

She gave him a serene smile. 'Trust me, Mr Alexander.'

'Trust is not a word I'd ever use where you're concerned,' he said coldly.

Georgina's eyes flashed. 'So we're back to that again, are we? If it's a battle of wills you're interested in, you've picked the right person. You won't wear me down. And do you know why? Because I'm innocent. If Craig did do you out of thousands he certainly never spent it on me. I wouldn't have let him, for one thing. Money doesn't interest me that much, not the way it does you. How many million are you hoping to make out of this little venture?'

He drew in a sharp breath. 'You make it sound as though money is a dirty word, and I find that rich coming from you. I don't believe your protestation of innocence.'

'Perhaps you should have asked Craig before shipping him abroad?' she countered hotly.

'Believe me, I did. I got the whole sorry story out of him. That's why I know you're telling me lies.'

'If Craig told you I was involved then he's the one telling the lies,' she riposted. 'And do you know what? I think you're the one who's to blame.'

Leon frowned harshly. 'And what's that supposed to mean?'

'He's lived with you since he was ten, isn't that right? And from what he's told me you've spoilt him rotten. You've done him no favours. Everything he does now is as a direct result of your upbringing.'

Leon snorted angrily. 'I taught him to be truthful and polite, to respect his elders, to——'

'But not to appreciate the true value of money,' she cut in acidly. 'I expect that everything he wanted he had. You got him accustomed to a lifestyle he couldn't possibly hope to afford once he was supporting himself.'

He drew in a sharp breath. 'You're talking about things which are no concern of yours.'

'They are when you accuse me of joining forces with Craig.'

'Not exactly joining forces, Georgina, but encouraging him to spend money on you that he hadn't got. If anyone's to blame for what he did, it's you, not me.'

Georgina did not want to listen to any more. It was clear he would never believe she'd had nothing to do with it. With an angry toss of her head she spun on her heel and marched into the next room.

Leon followed and came up close behind her. 'What a firebird you are. One can't help but wonder whether you're as passionate in other ways.'

She turned in alarm, her eyes flashing green fire. 'You'll never find out.'

His eyes narrowed. 'You shouldn't challenge me, Georgina. That's one thing I can never resist.'

'You touch me and I'll——'

She got no further; his arms slid around her and she was pulled hard against him. He looked deep into her eyes for a long, breathless second during which she tried unsuccessfully to free herself, her heart beating a frantic tattoo within her breast. No matter how he treated her it was impossible to ignore his sensuality. Maybe if she had not had a taste of it in the beginning it would have been different.

But she was not going to submit easily. 'You swi——' she began, her words cut off as his mouth claimed hers.

Georgina expected bruising hardness, a brutal punishment, but no, his lips were soft, moving expertly and sensually, the tip of his tongue moistening her lips, probing, opening them, the kiss deepening, and all within a matter of seconds.

Her heart-rate quickened dramatically, her throat contracted as her breathing deepened, and she felt a soft, unexpected moan escape her. There was already a deep ache in her groin and she could not believe that she was responding so instantly and so intensely and so excitedly to a man who despised her.

And what was he doing kissing her when he distrusted her so much? What game was he playing? She ought to stop him, but she was enjoying it too much. Craig had never aroused her in this fashion, but then she hadn't loved Craig. Craig was her friend. But neither did she love this man! He was despicable. He was using her, he was treating her like a slave. She was here to do his bidding, and it looked as though it was in more ways than one.

As this thought flashed through her mind she pushed against him with all her strength. But it was like pitting herself against a brick wall. He was immovable. 'You're wasting your energy,' he muttered, and his mouth fixed on hers again.

This time his hands slid beneath her jumper and while one warm, firm hand held her prisoner against him the other stroked the softness of her skin. Georgina knew she ought to stop him but hadn't the will. He was creating so many feelings inside her, sensations that she had never before experienced, that her whole body became sensitised, responding to him against her will.

What would have happened if Angus hadn't called out Georgina did not know. Leon stopped and looked at her with amusement in his eyes. 'That's definitely an experiment I'd like to repeat.' But then it changed to scorn. 'You didn't fight me very hard. Something tells me you were enjoying it. If you think that's one way to get round me, then forget it. All it does is confirm my opinion of you.'

'Enjoying it?' she derided, tugging her jumper straight. 'As I would kissing Dracula.'

At that moment Angus appeared in the doorway, 'Och, there you are, Mr Alexander. Can I see you for a wee minute?'

Leon nodded and crossed to the door. 'Can you carry on without me, Georgina?'

She smiled sweetly and falsely. 'I'll try.'

'Good. I'll see you later.'

Georgina's concentration was too disturbed for her to work; her mind kept coming back to Leon's kiss. She could still feel his mouth on hers, their bodies touching, the hardness of him, his strong, male smell. She only had to shut her eyes and he was there, arousing her, thrilling her.

She stood at the window, looking out but seeing nothing, and this was how Leon found her. 'What the hell are you doing?'

She swung round, though why she should feel guilty she did not know. 'As a matter of fact, I'm thinking,' she told him defensively.

'About the work you're supposed to be doing? Or what's just happened between us? No, don't tell me, it's clear by your face. But don't ever think that I'm softening towards you. I enjoyed kissing you, I won't deny that, and I'm not saying I won't do it again, but you won't ever get through to me that way.'

'I wouldn't dream of trying,' she replied coolly. 'You're not the type of man I'd pick as a prospective husband.'

His thick, arching brows rose. 'So what would he need to possess, this ideal man, except money, of course?'

Georgina's eyes flashed. 'Money doesn't enter into it.'

'So you keep telling me, but only the guilty protest too much.'

'Oh, you're impossible.' Georgina swung away and cast her eyes around the room, writing something in her notebook though she did not know what.

'I think it's time we called a halt for lunch.'

Her eyes widened. 'Don't tell me I'm allowed to eat?'

'Only because I need to get the best out of you,' he jeered. 'I don't want you fading away.'

His tone was mocking but Georgina felt sure there was more than an element of truth behind his words. She lifted her chin. 'What time do you want me back?'

'You're coming with me.'

'I am?' she frowned. 'Where to?'

'The inn in Stramore.'

She said no more, accompanying him from the building and sliding into his car. In the confined space she felt even more aware of him. She wished he hadn't kissed her; it made their business relationship very difficult. Even though it meant nothing to him she found it impossible to push the experience from her mind. Men were too casual about such things—they didn't suffer the same emotions as women. And she felt it even more because of the way they had been at their first meeting. He had seemed so sincere then. She could not believe he had changed so much.

The car was a brand new BMW, though whether it was hired or he had bought it to run around in while he was here she did not know. Probably he had bought it. He seemed the type to do just that.

'What are you thinking?' he asked abruptly, the low growl of his voice setting her nerves on edge.

'The truth?'

'Of course.'

'I was wondering whether this was your own car or a hired one.'

Georgina. Admittedly they were talking about work, but did he have to use that soft, sensual, toe-curling growl? Did he have to look at her so much and so often as though he could not get his fill of her? The exact same way he had looked at her that night of the cocktail party! Georgina refused to accept that what she felt was jealousy. She ought to be thankful that she had not got more deeply involved with him. He was clearly a man not to be trusted as far as the female sex was concerned.

'Iain tells me you might want some help.' Isabel Stewart, small and cheerful with black curly hair like her husband, paused at Georgina's side. 'If he can't give you the information you need then I'm certain I can. Come and see me any time.'

'Thank you,' said Georgina, liking the woman on sight, grateful for her intervention. 'I certainly will.'

'It's an enormous task you've got, but I envy you. I've never had enough money to refurbish even one room from scratch.'

'Nor me,' admitted Georgina. 'But it's different when you're using someone else's money.'

'I expect you to do your sums carefully,' cut in Leon, his tone abrupt.

Georgina had not even known he was listening. She had thought he was totally taken up with his blonde secretary.

'I have a budget worked out and I want you to stick to it.'

Isabel looked guilty and left and Georgina said with exaggerated politeness, 'But of course, that's the way I always work.'

'Sheena has it to type out now. I will let you have a copy.'

Their meal finished, Leon insisted she accompany them upstairs to the room he was using as an office.

Georgina presumed it was normally a bedroom—probably next to his!

Sheena's desk was face to face with Leon's. It was the only way they had been able to accommodate them both in the small room. Leon's desk was empty except for a pink folder. Sheena's on the other hand held her typewriter, a vast quantity of papers, and a dictaphone. Where the desks joined stood two telephones. Even as they entered one of the phones rang. Sheena spoke into it. She had a husky voice that was as sexual as Leon's growl. 'It's for you,' she said to Leon. 'Jim Reid of Puter Software.'

He had scarcely begun speaking when the other phone rang. Sheena answered and told the caller that Leon would ring back.

'Is he always this busy?' asked Georgina, recalling the two occasions his car phone had rung on the short drive to the airport.

'Always,' confirmed Sheena. 'He's a fantastic man, don't you think? I wish this were a permanent job; I've never worked for anyone like him. He's so wonderful, so clever. Have you known him long?'

'No, I haven't,' admitted Georgina. 'I'm here to do a job the same as you.'

'He's a hard worker.'

'And he expects the same of everyone else,' commented Georgina drily.

'Sheena,' cut in Leon, 'take a letter to Jim Reid.'

He dictated quickly and fluently and the girl's pencil flew over the paper.

'Always get everything down in writing,' he told Georgina when he had finished. 'Never rely on the spoken word. Remember that when you're getting quotes and estimates for the work done on Stramore House.'

Did he think he was talking to an imbecile? wondered Georgina, at the same time nodding her head. 'I always do, Mr Alexander. Could I possibly have a word with Isabel before we leave? I think she might be of more use to me than Iain.'

'Isabel's busy cooking dinner.'

'The dining-room is empty.'

'Bar meals,' he informed her succinctly.

'Then when would be the best time to see her? I want to get samples and brochures as soon as possible.'

'Sheena will fix something up.' He looked expectantly at the girl, who nodded.

'Now I think we should be getting back.'

'A Mr Wilson rang,' put in Sheena quickly.

Leon nodded. 'I'll ring him later.'

Georgina said, 'If you're busy, I'll walk.'

'I'm no busier than normal,' he told her brusquely, and in his car he said, 'What were you two girls twittering about?'

Georgina tensed, then thrust at him coldly. 'Sheena was singing your praises, Mr Alexander.'

'Was she, now?' A satisfied smile curved his lips. 'She's a nice girl, competent too. Don't you think it's about time you called me Leon? How can I kiss a girl who calls me Mr?'

'I'd like to think it was a deterrent,' she told him haughtily. 'I don't want you to kiss me again.' Especially now she had seen him with Sheena!

'Liar!'

She was astonished at the amusement in his voice and said at once, 'Is kissing me part of the contract? Doesn't it bother you that you're kissing the same girl as your nephew?'

A shadow darkened his brow. 'I wish you hadn't reminded me of Craig.'

'Why? If it will stop you kissing me then I'm glad I did.'

'Craig's a boy,' he snorted. 'He knows nothing about women. He thinks money will buy their friendship. He's a fool. He has a lot to learn.'

'And who taught him that?' she asked heatedly. 'He must have got the idea from someone. He was at an impressionable age when he came to you. And now, the first thing he's done wrong, and you wash your hands of him. Don't you think this is a time when he needs you to advise and guide him?'

Leon frowned harshly. 'He's lucky I didn't call in the police. I've brought him up to the best of my ability, and this is all the thanks I get.'

'This brother of yours in Texas, what's he like? Is he as hard-bitten as you?'

His frown deepened, carving his brow into two deep furrows. 'And what is that supposed to mean?'

'It means you have no heart.'

'I put Craig out of temptation's way, that's what I did,' he retorted coldly.

Georgina's brows rose. 'Really? Why didn't Craig go and live with him when his parents died, instead of you? It's obvious you have no love for him.'

Leon's knuckles gleamed white on the wheel and Georgina had the feeling that he would love to get his hands around her neck. 'It was discussed, obviously,' he said harshly, 'but my brother was newly married and had just bought the ranch. He didn't want a ten-year-old tearaway ruining his wedded bliss.'

'It might have been a better place to bring up a boy.'

'Craig never complained,' he grated. 'I did my best to keep him entertained. It was difficult at times, I was a young man myself, intent on building up a business empire. But I made sure I had time for him. I attended the necessary school functions, I helped him with his homework, I took him to football and cricket matches. We had fun together. And when I suggested he join me in the business he raised no objections.'

'How about his grandparents?' persisted Georgina. 'Aren't they alive?'

A muscle tensed in Leon's jaw. 'My father left my mother when Harry and I were still at school. She's married again now but has emigrated to Australia.'

The recollection still clearly upset him. So he did have a heart! Surprising! 'What sort of a job is Craig doing now?' she asked.

Leon threw off the memory and grinned. 'He's a ranch hand.'

Georgina lifted her brows. The contrast with trainee accountant was ludicrous. 'What does he know about cattle?'

'Not a thing, but he'll learn. A bit of good, hard, healthy outdoor work never hurt anyone. It should make a man of him.'

'You mean your brother's doing the job you should have done?' she said bitterly. 'How long have you banished him for?'

Leon's mouth tightened at her accusing words. 'Does it matter to you?'

'I care about Craig,' she said. 'He's a nice boy.'

'Oh, very nice,' he drawled. 'Any boy would be nice if he were showering you with gifts.'

'I blame you for encouraging him to spend money he hadn't got,' she flashed, and because she could see a full-scale argument developing she changed the subject. 'Are you going to give me the pleasure of your company for the whole afternoon?'

A quick, derisive smile curved his lips. 'Unfortunately, no, I have a meeting with the architect. Isn't that a pity?' And after a moment's pause, 'It might be a good idea for you to meet him. There are one or two things I want changing and it could affect your calculations.'

The moment they arrived back at Stramore House Georgina jumped out of the car and went indoors without waiting for Leon. She was finding it difficult to spend any length of time with him without her body responding to his. Whatever they were talking about—or arguing about!—his sensuality came through more strongly than anything else, and her body recognised it and acted on it—of its own free will! And she did not want this to happen. Her initial concept of him had changed. She no longer wanted anything to do with him on a personal or physical level.

It took a long while for her body to quieten down and she was sitting on the floor in one of the bedrooms, notepad in hand, pen poised, but thinking about Leon, when he came to find her. 'How industrious you are,' he sneered. 'Is this what I'm paying for?'

Georgina had not heard him come into the room and his hard words had her scrambling to her feet. 'A certain amount of this job, Mr Alexander, goes on in the mind,' she defended.

'By the look on your face it wasn't interior design that was occupying your thoughts.'

'You're right, it wasn't. As a matter of fact, I was thinking about you.'

A quizzical brow rose.

'And they weren't particularly pleasant thoughts.'

He looked taken aback by her brutal honesty but before he could comment she said, 'Has the architect arrived? Perhaps we should go downstairs?' And she walked out of the room.

She felt his eyes on her as he followed and a tingle ran down her spine. 'Are you always so blunt, Georgina?'

'If need be.'

'You could hurt a lot of people's feelings.'

'But not yours, I'm sure,' she said acidly. 'You have the hide of a rhinoceros.'

'What have I done to give you that impression?'

She turned and faced him. 'What have you done? For one thing, if you had a conscience you wouldn't have put me in that isolated cottage. Anything could happen to me.'

'Are you complaining?' A gleam lit up the steel-grey of his eyes.

'On the contrary, I like it. You might have thought yourself very clever tracking me down and insisting I do this job, but you clearly didn't find out what sort of a person I am. I don't get put down easily, I'm a fighter and I'm very resilient. Believe me, I had to be with three brothers like mine.'

He folded his arms across his hard-muscled chest. 'Maybe I have underestimated you. But there are other ways I can make your life difficult. For instance I could persuade your employer that you've fallen down on the job, perhaps even make you unemployable elsewhere— except by me!'

Georgina gasped. 'You're insane!' Not only was he insane, he was inhuman.

'An eye for an eye and a tooth for a tooth.'

'But you're already punishing Craig; why take it out on me as well?'

'Because he did it for you. It's that simple. You obviously encouraged him.'

'Rubbish! If he did it, he did it for himself.'

'Then why did his embezzlement only begin after he'd met you?'

Georgina frowned. 'How do you know that?'

'Because I had your affair checked out. I never pass judgement without getting my facts right.'

To give him his due Georgina believed him, but there had been no reason for Craig to take money from his uncle's company to give her a good time. She had never made any demands on him. Whatever he had given her, wherever he had taken her, had always been his own choice. It didn't make any sense.

'I can't explain it,' she said. 'I'm innocent, that's all I know.'

'How many criminals have said that?' he sneered.

'I have never been guilty of a crime in my life,' she thrust furiously. 'Really, Mr Alexander, you're making a big mistake. I suggest you have another talk to your nephew.'

'I will—one day. Meanwhile—you're here and Craig isn't, so——'

'So you're going to take your wrath out on me?' she interjected fiercely.

'As you were his—what shall I say?—partner in crime, though I accept you didn't have any part in the actual act of taking the money, I think I'm within my rights.'

'Rights be damned!' she cried, and then just as suddenly subsided and began to laugh. There really was a funny side to the situation—she was enjoying herself!

He frowned. 'Perhaps we should both share the joke?'

'You already know it, but I don't think you find it funny. Isn't that someone calling you?'

Georgina was grateful for Robert Lacey's interruption but her smile faded as they went downstairs to find him.

Leon's threat to tell Valerie that she was not doing her job properly worried her. Not only from the point of view that Valerie would lose money on it, but if she lost her job then she would lose her credibility as a designer also. She was still making a name for herself. He could do her untold damage.

Maybe she ought to ring Valerie and put her in the picture, tell her what he was like, give her side of the story first. But it wasn't that easy. There was no phone here yet, nor at the cottage, and at the inn there was a chance she might bump into Leon.

Robert Lacey was younger than Leon and less powerfully built but he had a genuinely warm personality. Blue eyes crinkled at the corners when he smiled, which was often, and his thick hair was enviably blond. He held her hand a fraction longer than necessary when Leon introduced them and Georgina felt his eyes on her often during their talks.

She did not mind. He was a very presentable young man and he made her feel good after the way Leon had spoken to her earlier.

'I think,' Robert said to Georgina, 'that we might need to liaise more. There **are** one or two other alterations to the original design. You do have a scale drawing? A couple of bathrooms slightly smaller, etcetera. It could affect your choice of sanitaryware.'

She nodded. 'Most definitely. If you have time once you've finished talking to Leon then perhaps we could get our heads together?'

'Absolutely, but I've an even better idea—let me take you out to dinner.'

'That won't be necessary,' said Leon abruptly. 'I don't believe business and pleasure should be mixed.'

'We'll do our talking first,' insisted Robert, 'unless of course I'm treading on your toes, Leon? I hadn't thought of that. Are you two...?' He paused and looked from one to the other.

'Not at all,' said Georgina with a quick smile. 'I'd love to come, Robert.'

Leon scowled. 'While Georgina's up here I feel responsible for her.'

'I'll look after her as you would yourself,' said Robert, clearly unable to understand Leon's reaction.

And Leon was left with no alternative but to give them his blessing. 'Make sure you do,' he growled.

Robert smiled but Georgina gained the impression that she would be made to pay for going out with Robert, and when she met the icy depths of Leon's eyes a shiver ran down her spine.

CHAPTER FOUR

GEORGINA had arranged to meet Robert Lacey in Stramore itself. Although he seemed gentlemanly enough she did not think it wise to let him know that she lived in an isolated cottage, but during the course of the evening she told him anyway and he was amazed that Leon should have insisted she stay there alone.

'You talk about Leon as though you know him well?' she frowned.

'Indeed I do,' he answered. 'I've worked on many projects with him.' He was wearing a casual summer shirt and they were sitting in a small, informal restaurant overlooking the loch. 'Are you sure there's nothing going on between you two? He actually looked jealous when I suggested taking you out.'

Jealous? Leon? That was a laugh! 'We most definitely have something going,' she said mischievously. 'I'm doing a job for him and he's determined to get his pound of flesh.'

'Leon doesn't believe in people slacking,' agreed Robert. 'But he's a workaholic himself so no one ever complains. That's not what I meant, though. Is there no—romantic link between you two?'

'There almost was,' she admitted, 'but something happened and there's nothing any more. Our relationship now is purely professional.' She took a timid forkful of haggis, having never tasted it before, not sure what to expect from this boiled mixture of sheep's heart, liver and oatmeal.

Robert watched her with interest. 'Do you like it?'

'It's not what I expected, but, yes, it's quite nice.'

'Quite nice,' he mimicked. 'Don't eat it if you don't like it, I'll get you something else.'

'I like it,' she said.

'Was there something more you wanted to know about Leon?'

Georgina nodded. 'I find him difficult to understand. For instance, why has he never married? He takes out enough girls and surely he must have met someone suitable?'

'He did once,' agreed Robert. 'He was even engaged. She worked for one of his companies, in quite a high position I believe.'

'So what happened?'

'She swindled him out of a lot of money.'

Georgina gasped.

'A surprise, eh? You didn't think he'd be foolish enough to let it happen?'

'How long ago was this?' The words came out with difficulty. She was finding it all a little too much to take in.

'Not long, a year, two at the most.'

'Oh! His nephew's done the same thing,' she said softly.

It was Robert's turn to look surprised. 'Is that so? Goodness me! It must have devastated him.'

'And I was his girlfriend, Craig's, I mean. Craig spun him some story about having a girl with expensive tastes. Leon banished him to the States, and now I'm here taking the brunt of his anger.' And why was she telling a complete stranger all this?

'I thought relations were rather strained between you,' said Robert. 'But surely you don't have to do the job? There are other interior designers.'

'He asked my employer for me particularly; he more or less forced her hand. He has a weird sense of justice.'

'I'll be around for a while,' said Robert gently. 'If you need a shoulder to cry on.'

'Thanks, but I'm not that soft,' she told him strongly. 'I can fend for myself, don't worry.'

He grinned and shook his head. 'You're quite a girl. But you will let me take you out again?'

'I'd like that,' she murmured, 'if you don't mind me sounding off about Leon now and then?'

'You feel something for him despite his attitude towards you?'

'I wouldn't be human if I didn't considering how attractive he is, but I can handle it.' She would have to, for Valerie's sake. She'd had time now to reflect on her earlier conversation with Leon and it would hardly be fair to drag Valerie into her personal problems at this stage. She would refuse to let him bully her, to push her around as though she were a nobody.

After they had finished eating they took a stroll along the side of the loch and Georgina looked up to where Stramore House stood on the towering hillside opposite. It was in an unrivalled position and Leon was right, it would be perfect for anyone wanting a holiday away from the rat race of modern society.

When Robert took her home Georgina discovered to her extreme annoyance that Leon's BMW was parked outside the cottage. What did he want now? Why was he here? Couldn't it have waited until tomorrow? Was he checking on Robert?

But when she pushed open the door it was empty and she asked Robert to stay for a cup of coffee.

He shook his head ruefully. 'I don't think so, not with Leon on the prowl. I like the guy, I really do, and I've no wish to invite any ill-feeling.' He touched his lips briefly to her brow. 'Thank you for coming out with me. I'll be in touch.'

Georgina furiously paced the room after Robert had gone, waiting for Leon, knowing he would appear, and within seconds he stood in her doorway. 'I don't need a watch-dog,' she snapped irritably, green eyes meeting grey.

'I just wanted to make sure you got home safely.' His tone was calm, a smile on his lips which did not reach his eyes.

'Well, I have, thank you. Goodnight.' She deliberately turned her back on him but he did not leave. Instead he stepped into the room and came towards her.

She felt the hairs prickle on the back of her neck and her anger deepened. 'You have a hell of a cheek, Mr Alexander,' she yelled, spinning to face him. 'You might have found me this cottage to live in but it doesn't give you the right to walk in whenever you feel like it.'

'Your door was open, you were obviously expecting me.'

'Only because your car was parked right outside. What were you doing, spying on us?'

'Really, Georgina, is that what you think? My conscience wouldn't let me stoop that low. But I am surprised Robert didn't stay.'

'He's a gentleman, Mr Alexander.'

'The name's Leon,' he reminded her. 'Did Robert kiss you?'

His complete change of subject was typical. 'I don't see that it's any business of yours,' she said coolly, her chin tilted, her red-brown hair a vivid flame of colour around her face.

'Perhaps I should have a word with him?'

'Telling him what?' She frowned.

'That you're my property.'

Georgina gasped. 'What a nerve. I don't belong to you, Mr Leon Alexander, not now, not ever.'

His hands came down heavily on her shoulders. 'If I were you, Miss Georgina Gregory, I wouldn't be too sure about that. When I make up my mind about something I rarely change it.'

She swallowed hard and met the cool greyness of his eyes. 'I think you're underestimating me. I'm a free agent. No one owns me, least of all you.'

The corners of his mouth lifted. 'Your fighting spirit is what I like best. But you're mine, Georgina, mine until I consider I've had fair recompense for the money Craig took.' His fingers moved beneath the heavy fall of her hair, reaching her nape, his thumbs stroking the soft skin behind her ears.

Frissons of sensation reached every nerve-end but she managed to stand still and calm, not giving herself away by even the flicker of an eyelash. 'I don't see how you can make that claim when I'm employed by Valerie Arden. I'm free to go back there any time I like. I don't have to stay here.'

His thumbs continued to caress and incite and he said, 'Oh, but you do. You no longer have a job with Valerie.'

Georgina gasped yet again and wrenched away from him, her eyes wide with shock. 'What are you talking about? Of course I've got a job.'

'Not since this afternoon,' he announced calmly. 'I telephoned Mrs Arden and told her that you wouldn't be going back, that you'd decided to work for me permanently. Naturally I've made sure she doesn't lose out financially. I know she's having a hard time in that direction. But . . .' He stopped when he saw Georgina's stunned expression. 'You don't believe me?'

'Oh, yes, I believe you.' Her voice was high with anger. 'It's just the sort of dirty, rotten, low-down trick I'd expect from a cunning swine like you. I hate your guts, and I don't intend staying here one second longer.' Her eyes flashed more green than they had ever been in her life, her whole body stiff with rage.

He smiled coolly. 'You won't get another job. I meant what I said about damning your reputation. You've no choice, Georgina. Run away from here and the word will be spread before you have time to catch your breath. I can do it, and you know I can.'

Her breasts heaved as she fought for control. Laugh, she told herself, laugh into his face, shatter his self-confidence, but for once her mother's advice failed to work. Instead she pounded her fists on his chest in stone-cold fury, and he stood and let her. It was as though he didn't feel a thing.

When she stopped, defeated, he said, 'Have you finished?'

'I think I might just stick a knife in your heart while you're asleep,' she snapped. 'That's if you do have a heart. Somehow I doubt it.'

'You hate me that much?'

'More than words can express. And as your opinion of me is rock bottom too I think that makes us about equal. It's not what you'd call a good working relationship, is it? I think you've made a very big mistake.'

His narrowed eyes watched her thoughtfully. 'I don't think so.'

'And what will I do once Stramore House is finished?'

'I like the idea of owning a group of country hotels. You and I between us will look for further suitable properties.'

He certainly did intend keeping her tied to his side, thought Georgina. 'How do you know this one will be a success?'

'I feel reasonably optimistic.'

'I could make a mess of the inside.'

'But you won't.' It was a threat rather than confidence in her work. 'And I don't want you going out with Robert again.'

Georgina shook her head. 'I don't believe this. You cannot rule my life completely. I'd like you to get out, *now*.'

'Not until you promise.'

'I'm promising nothing. I know you're doing your best to ruin my life but my friends are my own affair.'

'Then perhaps I ought to make sure that you prefer me to him?'

She knew what his intentions were before he reached her, and her heart skittered as she backed away. But there was nowhere to go. Her fingers sought the cold wall behind and her eyes met his contemptuously. 'This is rich. You come here in case I need protection from Robert and now you're the very one who's doing the assaulting.'

'I assault no woman,' he told her tersely.

'What do you call it, then, if she's not willing?'

'But you are. It's only your mind that has an aversion. Your body is responding to mine even now.'

He was right, damn him! But Georgina jutted her chin and glared. 'If this is the way you get your kicks then I feel sorry for you.'

Immediately he came to a halt. 'You're right, it is foolish. There's no fun in kissing a woman who doesn't respond. I'll wait, and next time I'll make sure that you're ready for me.'

'Which will be never,' she slammed, as he walked with a swagger towards the doorway.

A chuckle came from deep in his throat. 'Never is a long time, Georgina. You'd do well to remember that.'

When he had gone she collapsed into a chair. He was the rudest, most arrogant man she had ever met. Helen had been right, there was no doubt about it. But she had no intention of letting him get away with it. He couldn't do this to her. She wouldn't let him. First thing in the morning she would phone Valerie and find out if what he had told her was true. She found it difficult to accept that she had lost one job and been given another without her knowledge. Surely it wasn't possible?

All that night Georgina tossed and turned, her mind filled with confusion. Why was this happening to her? She had asked for none of it. She had done nothing. How could he lay the blame on her for something she had not done? What kind of a monster was he? Nothing made any sense any more. She ought to have guessed from the moment he insisted she do this job that it wouldn't work out.

She had so loved her work before all this happened. She had loved the variety and the freedom to create. No client had ever treated her as badly as Leon. And now he was saying he wanted her to work for him permanently, to join forces in buying new properties and turn them into first-class hotels. It just wasn't on. She wasn't used to working under this kind of pressure. He was breathing down her neck every second of the day. If Leon were different, more like the man she had first met, then she would have been deliriously happy. But now—under these circumstances...? It didn't bear thinking about.

At nine the next morning Georgina marched down into Stramore. While out with Robert last night she had spotted a telephone kiosk and it was towards this that she headed.

When Valerie answered Georgina took a deep breath and let fly. 'This is Georgina, Valerie. That man's a monster. I can't stay with him a moment longer. He's impossible to work with. I'm coming back.'

There was silence for a moment and then Valerie said, 'Georgina, please, do calm yourself. I understood from Mr Alexander that you wanted to be released from your job here with me? He said that——'

'*I* wanted it?' echoed Georgina in disgust. 'That's a lie! He made the arrangements behind my back. He presented me with a *fait accompli*. He told me I now work for him. Is that true?'

'Well—yes—sort of—I suppose. He said it was what you wanted. I thought it rather——'

'It is not what I wanted,' cut in Georgina furiously. 'He made it all up. I hate him. I refuse to work for him. I want my job back with you.'

Another long pause, and then Valerie said, 'I'm afraid it's not that simple, Georgina.'

Georgina frowned. 'What do you mean?'

'It's all cut and dried. Your employment with me has been terminated.'

'But you can't do that without my consent.'

'Oh, Georgina, I've done it. He paid me handsomely for the loss of business and I really did think it was what you wanted. He was very convincing.'

'I bet! Can't you give him his money back?' asked Georgina faintly, a feeling of doom spreading over her. She knew what Valerie's answer was going to be.

'If I do I'll lose the commission altogether and be forced into bankruptcy. I'm sorry, Georgina.'

'I'm sorry too,' she muttered, her mind searching wildly for another way round it but coming up with nothing.

'He put it all across so charmingly,' said Valerie. 'He convinced me you were happy there. Oh, Georgina, I really am sorry. Is it that bad?'

Because she did not want to worry Valerie any more Georgina swallowed the lump in her throat. 'I'm sure I'll cope. It was such a shock, that was all, to be told he was now my employer.'

'He's a fine man, Georgina. I think you under-estimate him. Give yourself time to really get to know him and things will work out.'

'Yes, you're probably right,' she sighed. 'I love the work, if nothing else. I'll just have to immerse myself into it.'

'You do that, Georgina. You're excellent at your job, you'll get on very well. Mr Alexander has many con-tacts; I'm sure he'll recommend you in all the right places.'

He also has the ability to ruin my reputation, thought Georgina, though she said none of this to Valerie Arden. It was her ambition, one day, to own her own design company—but it looked as though that idea was being knocked on the head before it had time to even see the light of day.

She walked slowly along the side of the loch, oc-casionally kicking the pebbles that crunched beneath her feet, wondering whether it really was worth putting up with Leon's harassment for the sake of her career. She believed him when he said he could ruin her reputation. He had the contacts and the power to either make or break her.

She had planned to go on working for Valerie for a few more years, gaining experience, making a name for herself, and then, when the time was right, start up on her own. She had seen no insurmountable problems to it—until Leon Alexander came into her life!

Quite why he was going to these lengths to keep her here she did not know. In one way she could understand his intention to give her a hard time—he really did think she'd had something to do with Craig taking that money. But surely this was taking things too far?

Without realising it Georgina had stopped and was staring up at Stramore House. If only Leon would go away and leave her to get on with the job. It wasn't necessary for him to remain. It hadn't even been necessary for him to set up an office here. It was all part of some diabolical plot to make her life a misery.

She began walking again and at the inn decided to call in and see Isabel. Sheena had fixed nothing up and time was passing. The woman proved invaluable, personally knowing people and suppliers who could be of help. Armed with her list Georgina went up to Leon's office. 'Can I use the telephone?' she asked Sheena. It was a major drawback that the cottage had no phone.

She sat at Leon's desk and made arrangements for representatives from various manufacturers and suppliers to come and see her. All the time Sheena watched her, and when she had finished the blonde girl said, 'Why does Leon spend all his time up at the house?'

Her tone was petulant, her eyes accusing, and Georgina could see that she was jealous. 'Because he always feels the need to supervise new projects,' she told her calmly. 'Before this it was a computer software firm down in the Midlands. He likes to keep his finger on the pulse until he's sure it's running satisfactorily.'

'So why has he got his office here instead of in the hotel?'

'Have you seen Stramore House?' asked Georgina with a smile. 'It's chaos. But I've no doubt he'll move in once all the structural work's finished and the phone's been connected.'

'How much time do you spend with him?' It was a lightly put question but Georgina knew how important the answer was to Sheena.

'Quite a lot, I suppose,' she admitted, 'but if you're wondering whether he's taking me out, then no, he isn't. We don't have that kind of a relationship.'

At that moment Leon himself entered the room. His eyes shot straight to Georgina. 'So this is where you've got to.'

She jumped to her feet. 'I've been making some calls. I saw Isabel this morning and she gave me a long list of people who might be helpful. But I've finished now. I'll get back.'

He nodded. 'If you wait for me I'll take you.'

With a gesture of resignation Georgina stood at the window while he gave Sheena instructions and took several phone calls. At last he was ready.

In his car he did not speak but Georgina felt the full impact of him, his nearness, his sexuality, all the feelings that had warmed her when they first met. There were times when they seemed to outweigh her hatred. It seemed that she would never get rid of this chemistry that had drawn her initially to him.

When he drove straight past Stramore House Georgina frowned. 'Where are we going?'

'I thought it was time you had some respite from your work.'

Her head jerked, her eyes watching him guardedly. This didn't sound like Leon.

'Just a ride to see the view, that's all. You've seen nothing yet of your surroundings.'

And whose fault is that? she wanted to ask, but wisely kept her thoughts to herself.

As the road climbed higher the views over the loch grew more magnificent. There was an island in the middle and Georgina wondered if anyone lived there. She supposed she could thank her lucky stars Leon hadn't thought of that instead of the cottage. She really would have been at his mercy then.

Finally he stopped the car and they got out. The road curved back around on itself here, following the promontory, and from their vantage point on the cliff-edge the view was unsurpassable. The loch glinting gold in the light of the sun, the sea beyond with its white-tipped waves, a fishing boat, gulls swooping and screaming, the forested sides of a distant mountain. Words could not describe how beautiful it was.

'It's like the end of the world,' whispered Georgina reverently.

'It does have a certain majesty,' he agreed. 'I've always liked Scotland.' His grey eyes narrowed on her. 'And do you know what, Georgina? I think I'm going to enjoy it even more now that you're working for me.'

There was something in his eyes which she could not quite fathom. He seemed to be looking right into her very soul, trying to find out what she thought deep down inside—almost as though it mattered to him!

Her heart suddenly pitter-pattered inside her breast and she swung away. It was her imagination. Leon had made it perfectly clear by both action and word that he was no longer interested in her. She was a victim of circumstances.

She turned and walked a distance away from him and as he did not follow she stopped and lifted her face to the wind, inhaling all the scents of the warm summer air, closing her eyes for a peaceful second.

That was her mistake. Leon came up silently behind her, so close they were almost touching. The hairs prickled on the back of her neck and she felt the power of him wrap itself around her. He seemed to be waiting for some signal, some sign that she wanted him to touch her.

The magic of the place enfolded them and all of a sudden this was a time of senses and needs and desires. But Georgina was afraid to let him know how deeply he affected her, how vulnerable she was where he was concerned, afraid that it might lead to something she was not ready for. He was a deeply disturbing man, for all his hardness, and she was not sure that she could handle him.

'What are we doing here?' She spoke the words aloud, softly, tentatively, not knowing whether he would hear, or even answer. 'What is it that you want from me?' And all the time her senses spun, every pulse raced with anticipation—and dread! It would be so easy to give herself away. She was living on a knife-edge, hating him and yet wanting him both at the same time.

The air around them was alive with electricity, every one of Georgina's nerves was excruciatingly sensitised. He was shatteringly close and she wanted to run away, to free herself of this torment, but was bound to him by invisible chains.

He did not answer her questions; instead he slid his arms around her waist, pulling her back against him. His touch sent a flood of impossible heat through her body, filling her with desire, and although she knew she ought to fight, to protest, to yell her anger, she did none of these things. He was once again the magnetic male animal she had first met. Their differences were forgotten. He was man, she was woman, and there was only one thing that they both wanted.

His hands slid up her trembling body to rest lightly on the soft fullness of her breasts. There was magic in his fingertips, magic that sent wave after wave of desire through her, and she made the shattering discovery that she wanted him to touch her, she wanted to feel their bodies pressed close together, she wanted to belong! It was corny saying that this was the man she had been waiting for all her life, but that was what it felt like. At this heart-stopping moment it was easy to forget the type of man Leon was and dwell only on what was happening to her body.

'I could be all things to you, Georgina.' His voice was a low, seductive growl, his hands moving sensuously over her curves, pulling her closer to him until their bodies fitted together like one. The hard length of his thighs sent a tremble through her limbs; she felt weak and disorientated, and could not believe this was happening to her. Her response was overwhelming. It had never happened to her before, not so strongly, not against her will.

His fingers slid beneath her blouse, grazing her soft skin, sending fresh tremors through her, inching slowly and achingly upwards, dispensing with the front fastening of her bra and taking the warm, ripe fullness of her breasts into his hands.

Georgina heard, as if from a distance, the soft, animal whimper that escaped her throat, her head fell back on his shoulder, and a trembling weakness invaded her limbs. Her body had a mind of its own, wallowing in the sensations he was able to arouse, wanting them, wanting more, needing fulfilment.

He turned her gently around, his fingers tracing her spine now, insidious, gentle movements designed to torment and incite. Her own hands reached out blindly, feeling the powerful ripple of muscle through the fine silk of his shirt, following each and every contour.

She looked up and met eyes that had darkened with desire, unaware that her own were mirroring the deeply violent emotions careering inside her. His mouth swooped on hers, swiftly, harshly, catching her by surprise, and yet her response was instantaneous.

Possessive hands pulled her savagely closer and Georgina melted against him. Her legs felt as though they were filled with water and she clung fiercely to him, unconsciously revealing the intense depths of her emotions.

His kiss deepened, his tongue exploring the soft, warm moistness of her mouth. Her throbbing heart raced out of control and she wondered if this was a turning point in their relationship.

But the thought lasted no more than a few seconds. Suddenly his hands dropped away from her and there was nothing but contempt in his grey eyes.

'What's wrong?' she asked in total bewilderment, the agony of her rejection showing in her eyes.

'Is your memory so short?'

The blood drained from her face as she stared at him uncomprehendingly. Her whole body grew cold and she wrapped her arms about herself in an effort to still limbs that were trembling now for a completely different reason.

'I promised you yesterday that the next time I kissed you you'd be ready for me.'

'Damn you!' Georgina choked.

'But I didn't realise how ready, or how far you'd be prepared to go. Did you think that if you offered me your warm little body things might change between us?'

The last traces of desire left her, but humiliation cut deep and she glared at him defiantly. 'I wasn't the one who started this. No woman in her right mind would get involved with you.'

'No?' he sneered. 'I could easily make you fall in love with me, Georgina Gregory. The temptation's already there.'

'You must be joking,' she scorned.

'So I was right, it didn't mean anything to you?' His eyes probed hers with unnerving intensity and Georgina realised she had fallen neatly into the trap he had set.

She had stupidly thought the kiss meant something to him, that he was actually beginning to see that she was not the bad lot he thought her. But no, it had meant nothing. Nothing at all. He did not care one jot about her. All he was interested in was cutting her down to size. In that moment she hated him, she hated him with every fibre of her being.

'I can see by your face that I'm right.'

The grim confidence almost had Georgina running away. But where to? They were miles from anywhere, she was completely at his mercy. There was no escape. He had forced her to accept his job if she wanted any sort of future for herself.

Forced her? How could he do that? What sort of simple-minded weakling was she? If she ran out on him now it wouldn't hurt Valerie. Her employer had already been compensated. All she would be doing was ruining her own chances of a career as an interior designer. But there were other jobs. He couldn't ruin her life altogether. 'I hate you, Leon Alexander,' she spat fiercely. 'I hate you, hate you, *hate you*,' and with that she turned and fled.

She expected to hear the pounding of footsteps, but nothing. And she did not dare turn and look. On and on she ran down the uneven track. If she could reach the road maybe she could thumb a lift? She could be well on her way back home to the Midlands before he even came to look for her. *If* he did. She was probably beneath his contempt and he wouldn't bother. How could she have kissed him like that, revealing how wantonly her body reacted to his? She should have known he would put the wrong interpretation on it.

She had almost reached the road when she heard the sound of a vehicle behind her. Twice in her haste she had fallen and grazed her knees, but now she ran even faster. It had to be Leon, it couldn't be anyone else. Could it? Perhaps help was at hand.

Stumbling to a halt, Georgina turned. Through the windscreen of the approaching car she could see Leon's shark-like grin. As she twisted away her heel caught in the uneven ground and with a cry she pitched forward right into his path. She could do nothing to stop herself. As if in slow motion she felt herself falling, saw Leon's look of horror, and heard the tortured squeal of brakes.

CHAPTER FIVE

How Leon missed her Georgina did not know. She lay there, paralysed with shock, waiting for the agonising impact, her whole body screaming out its fear, the screech of brakes sounding louder and louder until they almost deafened her. She actually felt the car's frightening nearness, the rush of air as it skidded sickeningly, miraculously, past her, and then the crashing of undergrowth as it slewed off the road.

Still she could not move. Silence surrounded her now; the car's engine had died, there was nothing but silence. *Silence? Leon! What had happened to Leon?*

She scrambled to her feet, charged with sudden, electric energy, and the scene that met her eyes brought fresh fear to her soul. The BMW had its nose buried in a tree-trunk and Leon was slumped, unconscious, over the steering-wheel.

Her trembling limbs were ice-cold as she waded through the bruised and broken bracken, following the path the car had taken. It was by her own stupidity that Leon was hurt. He could even be dead! *Dead!* The horrifying thought made her feel sick. Oh, God, she prayed silently, please don't let him be dead. *Please.*

She reached the car but the door would not open, no matter how much she tugged and pulled. Through the window she could see blood trickling down Leon's face. In a panic she clawed her way round to the other side and, relief, the door opened after a struggle.

'Leon! Leon!' No answer. She felt the pulse at his temple and it was strong. Relief flooded through her.

He was alive! *Alive!* She had to get help. She dared not move him in case anything was broken.

But as she backed out of the car he began to stir. He moved slowly, as though he were coming out of a deep, drugging sleep. His heavy lids lifted and his eyes tried to focus as he sat back in his seat and held a hand to his brow.

Then he saw her and she could see memory returning. 'You damn fool!' he grated and there was no weakness in his voice. 'I could have killed you.'

And I could have killed you, she thought agonisingly.

'Have you nothing to say?'

'I'm sorry,' she whispered.

'Sorry be damned. Why the hell did you run away?'

'You're hurt,' she said, deliberately ignoring his question. 'I must get help.'

He touched his fingers to his brow and looked frowningly at the fresh blood on them. 'It's nothing.'

But she could see the pain in his eyes. He was lucky the force of the impact had not shot him through the windscreen. Coming after her, he had not bothered to fasten his seatbelt. 'You're in no condition to walk,' she said.

For the first time he looked out of the windscreen and saw the crushed bonnet. He turned the key in the ignition and nothing happened. His face darkened. *'Damn you!'* he said thunderously.

'I'll go for help.' Again she attempted to back out of the car but his hand clamped down on hers.

'We'll go together.'

'You're in no fit state.'

'I have no intention of being held responsible if anything happens to you. You're going nowhere without me.' He let go her hand and reached out for the door-handle.

'It's stuck,' she told him needlessly.

With a further exasperated snarl he climbed over and out her side. There were beads of perspiration on his brow by the time he was standing and he steadied himself for a moment against the car.

'I don't think this is a very good idea,' she said in concern.

'I'll be all right,' he savaged, but he staggered like a drunken man as he made his way through the undergrowth and his pallor was alarming.

'Hold on to me,' she said, sliding her arm around his waist.

With reluctance he draped an arm across her shoulders and together, Georgina taking most of his weight, they managed to reach the road.

There were mixed feelings inside her. On the one hand she was desperately worried. If they had to walk far he would never make it; she could tell by the glazed look in his eyes that he was in constant pain. And he was right to blame her. She had been an idiot.

But she was also intensely aware of the man who had just kissed her. Nothing, it appeared, could quell the flame that had risen inside her. Feeling the heat of his body, feeling his heavy arm about her shoulders, his closeness, his sensuality even in this time of pain, all joined together to arouse her desire.

'Let's rest,' she said softly.

'I can make it,' Leon gritted.

'But I can't,' she lied. 'You're heavy.'

And so they sat on the grass verge and Leon leaned against a tree-trunk and closed his eyes. Georgina held a handkerchief to the gash above his eyebrow and to her amazement he did not knock her hand away. There was no traffic on this still summer afternoon. They sat there for a quarter of an hour and Georgina thought he had gone to sleep, until suddenly the drone of an engine sounded in the distance and he opened his eyes.

With a superhuman effort he got to his feet. Georgina offered him her arm but he ignored it. When the car came into sight he was standing in the middle of the road. Georgina could not help wondering what would happen if the car refused to stop.

But the grey vehicle slowed to a halt and the driver got out—a tall, elderly man with steely grey hair and silver-rimmed spectacles. 'Young man, if you stand in the middle of the road like that you're...' And then he saw Leon's bleeding brow and the whiteness of his face. 'What's happened?' He looked frowningly at Georgina who was now standing beside Leon.

'We had an accident,' she said, before Leon could speak. 'Our car's down that lane. Do you think you could give us a lift to the nearest hospital?'

The man nodded. 'Yes, of course. Your husband looks as though he's in a state of shock. I don't think he should be walking about.'

'I'm not her husband,' shot Leon loudly, 'I'm her employer, and I'm perfectly capable of walking, thank you very much. And I don't need a hospital, I just want to get back to Stramore.'

The man's brows rose and he glanced at Georgina sympathetically.

She gave a wan smile. 'You're very kind. We really appreciate you stopping. Please go to the hospital.'

'Georgina!' roared Leon. 'I don't need any treatment.'

She shrugged and looked at the man. 'I'm sorry, perhaps you could take us to Stramore?' And then she would call a doctor.

They both climbed into the back of the car and Leon leaned his head against the seat and closed his eyes again. Georgina sat and watched him.

'What happened?' asked the man.

Georgina knew she could not tell him she had been running away without making herself look foolish. 'The car skidded off the road,' she said, hoping he would ask no further questions, 'and smashed into a tree.'

'I'm surprised you weren't hurt too.'

Georgina did not answer and within ten minutes they reached the inn. 'You're very kind,' she said to the man, hanging back as Leon walked unsteadily inside. 'I was worried sick that no one would come along.'

'I was once in a similar situation,' he said, 'and no one stopped to help me. I'm glad I could assist. I hope your—employer will soon recover. I really think he should see a doctor.'

Georgina nodded. 'I'm going to arrange it.'

Inside she told Iain what had happened and asked him to phone for the doctor, and then she went up to Leon's room. Hesitantly she tapped on the door, but as it was open she walked inside. 'What were you and that man talking about?' he growled. He had stripped off his shirt and was holding a clean towel to his forehead.

'Nothing. I was just thanking him for his kindness.' Leon had a magnificently tanned chest, deep and muscular with a scattering of dark hairs. Looking at him almost took her breath away.

'It took you that long?'

Georgina felt her anger growing. 'What is this, Leon, a third degree? The man was merely concerned for your health. I thought he was very kind.'

'And very rich? I'm sure it didn't escape your notice that he drove a Mercedes.'

'Your thoughts stink,' she snapped. 'Here I am worried sick about you and all you can think about is that I might be trying to get off with some other man.'

'You? Worried? About me? Now why would that be, I wonder?'

Georgina swung away and would have left the room if he hadn't called her peremptorily back. 'Wait! Go and ask Sheena to phone the garage, get them to tow the car in, and have another car brought around at once. Then come back and dress this damn wound.'

With a bit of luck the doctor would be here before she had finished talking to Sheena, thought Georgina, slipping thankfully out of the room.

His secretary was horrified and wanted to go rushing to him, but Georgina detained her. 'The doctor will be here in a minute, meanwhile Leon needs to be quiet.'

'How did the accident happen?'

Again Georgina was reluctant to divulge the whole truth. 'The car skidded off the road.'

'But how? Why? Was Leon speeding?'

'It was only a lane, and the road surface wasn't very good.'

'In that case I'm sure Leon wouldn't take risks. He's a very careful driver.'

It was obvious Sheena thought Leon could do no wrong. 'He had to brake quickly.'

'What for?'

Georgina sighed heavily. 'If you must know, he was coming after me. I'd run away, and then I slipped and fell right in front of the car.'

Sheena's eyes widened. 'He could have killed you. Did you have an argument?'

'Sort of.' How could she tell Sheena that it was because he had kissed her?'

'How could you fall out with a man like Leon?' Sheena's eyes became dreamy. 'I'd never argue with him, ever.'

But you wouldn't like it if he accused you of kissing him for mercenary reasons, thought Georgina.

And then Sheena frowned accusingly. 'What were you two doing out together anyway? I thought you said there was nothing going on?'

'That doesn't stop him trying to kiss me,' shot Georgina, feeling a sudden urge to put this girl in her place. 'Excuse me, I think I hear the doctor.'

Leon's face reddened with rage when he saw Dr Campbell and he glared at Georgina accusingly. 'I told you I wanted no doctor,' and to the man himself, 'You're wasting your time.'

The man smiled soothingly. 'You look as though you've had a nasty bump—I may as well take a look now I'm here.'

Leon continued to grumble as the doctor cleaned and dressed the wound which was already swelling alarmingly. Fortunately the cut wasn't deep and only needed a light dressing.

'You're very fortunate it isn't a lot worse,' said the doctor when he had finished. 'If you have any problems don't hesitate to come and see me.' And to Georgina, 'I'd like a word with you, please.'

In the corridor outside he said, 'You're his secretary, did he say? Is there a wife around? Is he married?'

'No.' Georgina shook her head. 'And I'm not his secretary. I'm simply doing a job for him.'

'But you're working together?'

'Most of the time, yes.'

'Good. He needs to be watched closely for the next forty-eight hours.'

Georgina nodded. There was no question now of her running away, not until Leon was better.

'If he has any excessive headaches or drowsiness let me know immediately.'

'Yes, Doctor, I'll do my best, though Leon isn't the type to complain. He'll soldier on as though nothing's wrong.'

'So I've gathered,' he said with a wry smile.

When Georgina went back into Leon's room he was lying on top of the bed and some of the aggression seemed to have gone out of him. 'What did he have to say?'

She stifled a smile. 'He wants me to keep an eye on you in case there are any after-effects.'

An eyebrow attempted to rise but his brow creased in sudden pain and for a moment he closed his eyes. 'And are you?'

'Am I what?'

'Going to look after me?'

'I don't think that's quite what the doctor had in mind. You don't need a nursemaid.'

'I wouldn't mind being pampered by someone as pretty as you.'

Georgina looked at him suspiciously but his face was as innocent as a child's.

'I'm hungry. Will you ask Iain to send up some sandwiches? And you may as well join me.'

'I don't think so,' she said. It was far too intimate here in his bedroom and she did not entirely trust him. 'I've already lost out on half a day's work. I really should get back.'

'I'm telling you to stay.' Although there wasn't the usual hard tone in his voice it was firm enough to brook no refusal.

'You're the boss,' she shrugged. 'What sort of sandwiches would you like?'

'Chicken, ham, I don't care. Just get going.'

She went down and found Iain and gave him the order. When she returned Sheena was with Leon.

She was bending over him on the bed and although she straightened when Georgina entered it was not difficult to guess that they had been kissing. Sheena had the look of a satisfied cat and Leon looked quite pleased with himself as well.

Georgina felt a shaft of jealousy shoot straight through her. It proved beyond any shadow of doubt that the kiss he had given her earlier had been nothing more than a test of her virtue. She had been a fool to read anything else into it, and even more of a fool to respond. She would be very careful not to give herself away in future. There would be no hint of the passion that raged inside her against her will.

'That will be all, Sheena,' he said softly.

The girl sauntered out, her hips swaying, casting Georgina a triumphant smile. If he can kiss you he can kiss me, it seemed to say.

Georgina felt uncomfortable in Leon's small room. The bed filled a very large part and with Leon stretched out on it he was the dominating factor. Near the window was a small round table and two chairs. She walked across and sat on one of them. 'Iain will send up the sandwiches as soon as they're ready.'

He nodded briefly and remained silent. Georgina looked at him worriedly. 'Are you all right, Leon?'

He smiled then. 'So it takes an accident to make you call me Leon.'

She shrugged, her lips twisted wryly. 'You look very vulnerable down there.' And then wondered at her daring.

'Will it be back to Mr Alexander once I'm better?'

'That depends on the way you treat me.'

'I'm wondering if putting you in that cottage by yourself was a good thing. I think you should be nearer to me.'

A swift frown furrowed Georgina's brow, and her heart jumped violently. The cottage was her refuge; she could go home at the end of her day's work and relax. There was no Leon to jump down her throat. She cherished the few hours she spent there. 'What have you got in mind?'

'I'm not sure,' he said lazily, an enigmatic smile curving his lips, softening the harsh lines of his face. 'There are several options open to us. You could take a room here—but that wouldn't be very convenient, it's too far from the house. On the other hand I could move into the cottage.'

'No!' Georgina's response was instantaneous. 'That wouldn't be very convenient either. It's too small, there's only one bedroom.'

'Correction, there are two. It wouldn't take long to knock the other one into shape. Does it worry you, the thought of me moving in with you?'

'I don't think it's a very good idea at all.' Especially as there was no bathroom. Stripping off and washing herself at the kitchen sink in front of Leon wasn't her idea of fun at all. 'Besides there's no phone. You'd be far better off staying here.'

'The third option is moving into Stramore House,' he went on. 'It shouldn't be long before some of it's habitable. In that way your privacy will be preserved!' His eyes mocked her. He knew exactly what she had been thinking! 'The phone's being reconnected within the next couple of days. What do you say to that?'

'Do I have a choice?'

'I'm perfectly willing to listen to your comments.'

But not to act on them, she thought. 'I think moving into the hotel sounds an excellent idea. Working on top of the job has to be good.' There was also the fact that there would be a shower and hot running water. It sounded like bliss.

'I think so too. I'll get it organised.'

At that moment Iain tapped on the door and entered with their sandwiches. León jumped up but was knocked back again by the pain in his head.

'Stay there,' said Georgina at once, already half on her feet.

Every vestige of colour drained out of his face, but within seconds, grimly determined, he was up again.

'You should do as you're told,' said Iain. 'You look terrible, man.'

'A little knock on the head's not going to confine me to my bed.' Leon growled. 'Pour the tea, Georgina. My throat feels like sandpaper.'

He joined her at the table and with a shrug and a grimace Iain left.

The bump had not spoilt Leon's appetite. He ate ravenously, pausing only to motion to Georgina to eat too. The chicken was tender, the bread thick and fresh, and it was accompanied by crisp lettuce and firm, red tomatoes. He drank two cups of tea and afterwards sat back in the chair and closed his eyes.

'If you don't need me I'll go,' said Georgina, rising to her feet. She still felt uneasy in this room.

His lids lifted and he surveyed her lazily. 'Why are you in such a hurry?'

'I've told you, I have work to do.'

'And I need you here.'

'If it's company you're craving then I'm sure Sheena will be only too delighted to oblige.'

'I'm sure she will, but I want you with me. You're good for me. You're unlike any other female I've met.'

His answer surprised her and her green eyes widened as she looked at him. 'You mean I speak my mind?'

He smiled slowly. 'There's certainly never a dull moment when you're around.'

'So you want me to stay and entertain you. Is that what you're saying?'

Still he smiled. 'I never thought of it as entertainment, but yes, I suppose you're right. Stay and entertain me, Georgina.'

'I don't think so. I think your entertainment would be my humiliation.'

'Do I humiliate you?'

She watched him closely. 'Ever since we met you've taken a perverse delight in doing everything possible to hurt me in some way or another.'

'Don't you think you've hurt me?'

'Because of Craig?' she frowned. 'Isn't it about time you forgot that whole silly nonsense? Haven't you seen for yourself that I'm not a girl with expensive tastes? I like the simple life. I like that cottage you found me. I don't crave jewellery and designer clothes and some man taking me out for over-priced meals and spending his every penny on me.'

He applauded mockingly. 'Well said, Georgina.'

'But you don't believe a word of it?'

A moment's pause, a moment in which his eyes never left her face. 'It might surprise you, but I'm beginning to.'

It did surprise her. In fact it stunned her.

'You're not quite the conniving bitch I expected.'

Her eyes widened. 'Well, thank you, Mr Alexander.'

'Unless of course it's all an act?'

'I'm no actress, I can assure you of that,' she said swiftly, still shocked by his admission.

'Then sit down and let us really get to know one another.'

Georgina's heart hammered along at an alarming pace. 'I don't think now is the time to talk. You should be resting. You should be in bed.'

'I will if you'll come with me.'

The glint in his eyes told her that he knew she would refuse. But she resumed her seat with dignity, feet together, her hands clasped in her lap. 'I think you'd have the biggest shock if I agreed. What shall we talk about?'

'Tell me about you. Tell me about your ambitions.' His smile was one of those warm, heart-stopping smiles that she had not seen for a long time. It rose goosebumps on her skin and sent tremors pulsing through her.

'Actually I can't see myself moving on. I seem to be— trapped!' She said the word with deliberate contempt, despite the feelings he had managed to arouse inside her.

'You're saying it's my fault?'

Georgina swallowed and nodded.

'OK. Tell me what you would like to do if you weren't working for me. If I released you.'

'Work hard, make a name for myself, start up on my own. It's what I've been aiming for for quite a long time.'

He inclined his head. 'An admirable ambition. I know the feeling. I had similar ones myself.'

Georgina could not believe he was being so nice to her. Perhaps the knock on the head had done him good? She could actually feel the rapport that had drawn them together in the first place. 'So how did you start?' It was something she had often wondered but never dared ask.

'Would you believe my first enterprise was a flower barrow in Covent Garden?'

Georgina smiled. It was difficult to imagine Leon doing something like that.

'I planned to be a millionaire by the time I was thirty.'

'And were you?'

He nodded.

'What sort of businesses do you own?'

He shrugged. 'A wide range. Flower shops, computer hardware and software, travel.'

'And now hotels?'

'That's right—and they can each be useful to the other.'

'You make my simple ambition sound very pitiful.'

'No, Georgina, don't say that. I admire career girls. Women have let themselves be put down for far too long. What I don't like is girls who let the power go to their heads. I think they should remain softly feminine and let themselves be pampered by men. I don't strictly believe in equality.'

'I have a friend who wouldn't like to hear you say that,' she smiled.

He put a hand to his head and Georgina could see the pain in his eyes. 'I really do think you should rest now, Leon. I'll go and do some work.' And this time he did not detain her.

As she closed the door Georgina felt that they had taken a giant step forward in their relationship, and when she arrived at Stramore House she was smiling. The first person she saw was Robert. 'I've been looking everywhere for you,' he said. 'How would you like to have dinner with me tonight?'

'I'm sorry, I have other plans,' she told him softly.

'Leon?' He looked regretful.

'No.' She shook her head. 'Actually I'm going jogging.' It had been a spur-of-the-moment decision as she walked up to the hotel. She was in just the right mood.

'I'll join you,' he said, much to her surprise. 'That's if you don't mind?'

'I don't mind at all.'

He grinned. 'What time shall we meet?'

'Seven o'clock here?'

'OK. And afterwards how about a light supper at my place?'

Georgina hesitated only slightly, recalling Leon's warning not to see Robert again. But he wasn't her keeper. Why shouldn't she see him? She smiled. 'Thank you, I'd like that.'

She spent the rest of the day making further copious notes and a man turned up from one of the carpet suppliers she had telephoned. She admired his eagerness to do business and decided that if the price and delivery were right he would be the one to get their order.

Back at the cottage she sat a while and reflected on the day's events. So much had happened—and her relationship with Leon had taken on a new slant, a whole new slant. He no longer blamed her for aiding and abetting Craig. She felt happy, deliriously happy, and sang to herself as she changed into shorts and T-shirt. She was still smiling when she met Robert.

They set off at a steady pace, Robert matching his stride to hers. 'I've been to see Leon. I didn't know about the accident. Sheena was with him. He's being well looked after.'

Some of Georgina's happiness faded but she deliberately kept her tone light. 'That's good. The doctor said he needed an eye kept on him. With bumps on the head you can't be too sure.'

'He didn't look too bad. How are you and he getting on? I understand you were out together when the accident happened?'

Georgina grimaced. 'I wouldn't like to say what the situation between us is. He took me for a ride and then we had an argument and I ran away. But since the accident he's been quite nice to me. Actually I think he's at last beginning to believe I didn't encourage Craig to take that money.'

'So things could look up?' He tried in vain to hide his disappointment.

She shrugged. 'Who knows what tomorrow will bring. He's so unpredictable.'

The subject of Leon was deliberately changed and they chatted and laughed and she told him tales about her brothers and he told her about his family and before they knew it they had jogged ten miles and were back at his flat.

It was a couple of rooms in an ordinary house in Stramore village but he had a shower and Georgina found it heaven to stand beneath the refreshing jets.

He provided her with a clean shirt and a pair of jeans which weren't a lot too big once she had fastened a belt around her waist and while he had his shower she continued the preparations he had begun for their supper.

The poached haddock, new potatoes and peas went down very well and they followed it with fresh raspberries and natural yoghurt, and afterwards Georgina said she ought to go. It wasn't fair on Robert to spend so much time with him, knowing how he felt about her, knowing she would never reciprocate his feelings. She had tried all evening to keep the atmosphere light and impersonal, but he had taken no steps to hide his very real attraction for her.

He walked her home and it was still daylight. Up here in the Highlands in midsummer it did not get dark until half past eleven. Georgina did not invite him in but in the doorway he asked whether he could kiss her.

She felt it would be rude to refuse so lifted her mouth to his. But there was none of the magic she now associated with Leon's kisses and Robert turned sadly away.

'I'm sorry,' she whispered.

'Don't be. I just hope that Leon doesn't hurt you. Will you be at the hotel in the morning?'

She nodded.

'I'll see you there, then. There are some points I wish to discuss with you.'

Georgina slept easily that night and actually looked forward to seeing Leon the following morning. What she hadn't expected was that he would come to see her! He turned up at the cottage before she had even finished her toast. His good humour of yesterday had gone. His brow was swollen, the bruise was turning purple around his eye, and he still had that glazed look that spelt pain, but on top of that he was visibly angry. 'I thought I told you I didn't want you to see Robert again?' he thrust harshly, walking in through the open doorway.

How had he known? Who had seen them and told him? Had he seen them himself? Was Stramore the type of village where everyone knew what was going on? Was nothing secret? Not that it really mattered, but she resented being told who she could date. 'You don't own me,' she snapped, 'and you shouldn't be here. You look far from well, you should be in bed.'

'I'll do what I damn well please,' he growled. 'What were you doing in Robert's flat?'

Georgina grinned suddenly and mischievously. 'Taking a shower. We were both hot and sticky after our jog.'

A sharp frown deepened the lines between his thick brows. 'Parading in front of him naked?'

'Would that bother you?' she asked lightly.

'Damn you, girl, have you no sense of decency?'

'I do what I please,' she told him, still with the light of mischief in her eyes.

'What else did you two do besides go jogging—and share a shower?'

There were lines of contempt in his eyes and Georgina's humour turned to anger. 'We went to bed and made love, what do you think we did?'

The moment the words were out she regretted them, especially when his eyes narrowed to slits and he sucked in a harsh breath. *'You slut!'*

Georgina flinched. 'God, Leon, you don't believe me, do you? We had a meal, that was all, and then he took me home.'

Bitter sarcasm hardened his voice. 'He didn't touch you, is that what you're trying to say? Goddammit, girl, Robert's a red-blooded male the same as the rest of us. And you're a very attractive woman.' He threaded his fingers through her burning chestnut hair and pulled her painfully towards him.

'Leon, you're hurting!'

'And I'll hurt a lot more if you don't tell me the truth.' His face was all hard lines and angles, his white teeth grating together, his eyes probing.

'The truth is Robert kissed me, and that's all,' she flung at him defiantly. 'Now let me go.' It felt as though he was trying to pull every hair out of her head.

'A kiss!' he sneered. 'A kiss is just a kiss, is that what you're saying? How did he kiss you? Like this?' And he kissed her briefly and perfunctorily. 'Or like this?' And now his mouth fixed on hers in a deliberate assault of her senses, going on and on until Georgina's head was reeling and her body throbbing.

'Tell me?' he demanded roughly.

'A quick goodnight kiss,' she whispered. 'Nothing like that.'

She thought she saw relief in his eyes but it was gone in an instant and she could not be sure. 'I hope you're telling me the truth?' he grated, finally letting her go.

Georgina rubbed her head with both hands, trying to ease the pain, glaring at him angrily. 'You'll believe what you want to believe, the same as always. The same as you believed Craig when he said I had expensive tastes.'

'He spent the money on someone.'

'Himself?' she suggested. 'His flash car?'

'I bought his car.'

'Then I don't know what he did with it. All I know is very little of it came my way. Robert said you'd been swindled before. Is that why you're so suspicious of everyone?'

'*Robert said?*' His face contorted with renewed anger. '*Robert?* It sounds to me as though you've had some mighty personal conversations considering you've only just met. In future I'd thank you not to discuss my private affairs with all and sundry—and I'll have a word with Robert myself.'

'You can't blame him,' she said at once. 'It wasn't his fault. How was he to know your disastrous love-affair was one big secret?'

His breath whistled out through his teeth. 'It's no secret, but I swore it would never happen again. I loved Anita, did you know that? I was actually stupid enough to fall in love, something I'd always sworn I would never do. It certainly taught me a lesson. I shall never let any woman get that close to me again.'

CHAPTER SIX

GEORGINA wanted to find out something more about this girl whose name was Anita. A girl who had stolen Leon's heart and then trampled on it. A girl who had hurt him so much he never wanted to fall in love again.

The hurt was still there in his eyes, a shadow that had nothing to do with the accident. 'Won't you tell me about it?' she suggested softly.

'I thought Robert told you?' he snarled.

'Not everything. Just that some girl had defrauded you. I can see now why you were so harsh on Craig. It must have been dreadful for it to happen a second time.'

'I don't want or need your sympathy,' he growled.

'I really would like to know.'

'I don't see what good it will do.'

'It might help me understand you a little better.'

He was silent a moment then he dropped down on to a chair at the table where Georgina's unfinished breakfast still lay. 'I suppose it will do no harm; better you know the true facts than whatever rumour is going around. I don't know why people can't keep their noses out of other people's business. Is there any tea in the pot?'

Georgina nodded and poured him a cup, adding milk but no sugar, topping up her own cup at the same time. 'Would you like some toast?'

'No, thanks.' He picked up the cup, cradling it in his hands, gazing into its depths as though it were a crystal ball, as though he was looking back in time, seeing the girl who was the cause of the bitterness that festered inside him.

Waiting for him to speak, Georgina remained silent, sipping her tea, forgetting now the toast that lay half eaten on her plate. She felt his presence strongly in this room. He overpowered it. He filled the air so that she felt she was breathing him in. There had been nothing like this with Robert last night.

'I met Anita at a conference. She impressed me with her business acumen and her flair for getting things across. She was presenting a paper on marketing strategy and the resultant increase in profits. I decided I wanted her to work for me.'

Just like that, thought Georgina. Had he ridden roughshod over her employer as he had Valerie? Had Anita had any choice in the matter? Or had the girl been willing? Had it been love at first sight? It amazed her how the thought of Leon making love to another woman hurt.

'She took some persuading. I had to offer her a far higher salary than I'd intended.' His lips compressed at this point. 'Perhaps I should have recognised then that money was the only thing that meant anything to her.

'I made her major accounts and sales manager for a communications company I'd only recently acquired. Because of earlier management mishandling profits had fallen drastically. In fact they were on the point of bankruptcy when I took over.

'Anita worked hard in the beginning, oh, yes. Profits not only crept up, they leapt up. I was very impressed. She was better than any man could have been. So impressed in fact that I began asking her out to dinner. Before I knew it I was hooked.' His mouth twisted bitterly at the memory and he lifted the cup to his mouth and drank the contents without stopping.

Georgina offered the pot and refilled it for him. She was frankly amazed that Leon was telling her so much.

She had expected at the most a very brief explanation, in fact she had expected him to tell her to mind her own business.

'Anita was a beautiful girl, Georgina. Long black hair, almost to her waist, huge brown eyes like those of a newly born fawn. Every man in the company fell in love with her. I was exultant that she chose me when she could have had any single one of them. I asked her to marry me and she agreed and I was the happiest man in the world.' His mouth tightened and his breathing grew noticeably deeper. 'I didn't know she was after me for my money.'

'Was that when she began to filter funds from the company?' breathed Georgina.

'God, no!' He rested his brow on a hand and closed his eyes. 'She was at it from the very beginning. So cunning, so clever. I never suspected. I was pleased with the way profits were going up. I never dreamt that a certain percentage were going into her own pocket. It wasn't until afterwards, until after I'd found out, that I discovered I wasn't the first fool to be taken for a ride. She used her looks and her brain to get exactly what she wanted. She skipped from job to job and never got caught.'

'So how did you find out?'

'A phone call from a business friend for whom she'd previously worked. His profits had shot up as mine did, but they increased even more after she'd left. He became suspicious and had some investigations carried out. They found out where the money had been disappearing from but there wasn't a single shred of tangible evidence. Nothing that could have stood up in court. Her method of working was very, very ingenious. It's about the only thing I admire her for.'

'So you got rid of her and since then you've never trusted another woman? Isn't that a bit extreme?'

'Only beautiful, clever women, Georgina. I use them as I was once used. It was a bitter lesson.'

'But we're not all alike.'

He looked at her then and there was something in his eyes that set Georgina's nerves jangling. For a fraction of a second he had bared his soul. He had let her see that he wasn't as immune to her as liked to make out. That she, like Anita, had got through to him. But he wasn't going to allow it, he was going to fight it every inch of the way.

And the knowledge lit a fire inside Georgina. It boosted her morale and she knew now that it was only a matter of time before he admitted feeling something for her. She wouldn't have to leave. She would stay, and wait, and hope, and one day... The thought warmed and excited her. She would help him, she would teach him that all girls weren't the same.

'Is your head hurting?' she asked gently as he rested his brow once more in his hands. 'Do you think you should see the doctor again?'

'No, I don't.' He lifted his head and looked at her, his eyes heavy with pain but his earlier anger gone. Talking about Anita had made him forget Robert—until Robert himself suddenly appeared in the doorway.

He did not see Leon at first. He tapped the door and smiled at Georgina. 'May I come in?' In his hand were her shorts and T-shirt that she had forgotten last night. 'I looked for you at the hotel. I thought perhaps you weren't well.'

Georgina glanced at her watch and was amazed to see it was twenty-five minutes past nine. Leon had been here over an hour. How the time had flown!

She caught Leon's eye and the black anger was back. He scraped his chair away from the table and stood up. At that moment Robert, coming into the room, saw him.

'Oh, I'm sorry, I didn't realise you were here, Leon. How are you this morning?'

'Wondering what the hell you were doing taking Georgina out last night.'

Robert was visibly shocked by this attack, but before he could speak Leon went on, 'I've said before I don't believe in mixing business with pleasure.'

'How dare you?' Georgina shot to her feet, her green eyes flashing. 'That's the most stupid thing I've ever heard. My seeing Robert in no way affects our work and if I want to see him then I will, and there's precious little you can do about it.'

Robert added his feelings to hers. 'Georgina's right, Leon. As we're both strangers to the area it's only natural we should feel drawn together. I see no reason why we shouldn't continue to see each other.'

They both omitted to say that their feelings were nothing other than platonic. He had angered them by trying to make out they were having some sort of sordid affair.

Leon frowned harshly from one to the other, his livid bruise making his expression even more fierce than it actually was.

'Your clothes, Georgina,' said Robert, putting them down on a chair. 'I'll see you later.' And with a final tight glance in Leon's direction he turned and left the room.

The silence that fell between them lasted no more than a few seconds and yet it felt like an aeon. Georgina was seething inside. The few minutes when she had actually felt close to Leon had gone. He had no right to speak to Robert like that, no right at all—unless—unless it was jealousy!

The thought shocked her the instant it was born. Shocked and thrilled. She would react in exactly the same way if he took Sheena out. The only difference being that she would not let him see how she felt. She would keep her feelings hidden, locked away from his too seeing eyes.

Yet when she looked at him there was nothing in his eyes to suggest that he felt anything for her. They were as hard now as two chips of granite.

'What was Robert doing with those?' he growled, looking down at her T-shirt and shorts on the chair.

Georgina shrugged and said sharply. 'Not what you're thinking. They were wet with perspiration after our jog— he lent me some clothes.'

'How kind!' he sneered. 'A most intimate gesture— for a stranger! I meant what I said about not wanting you to go out with him again.'

'And *I* meant what *I* said. You can't stop me!'

Their eyes met and the hostility in the air filled the tiny room, making it difficult for Georgina to breathe. She jutted her chin and matched his hardness. 'If you wouldn't mind leaving I'll clear away and get to work.'

'So that you can see Robert again?'

She refused to be drawn into further argument.

'You do realise that he won't be here much longer? His work is very nearly finished.'

Georgina felt regret. She would be losing an ally. She would have no shoulder to cry on. But it wouldn't break her heart.

'Are you going down to the hotel as well,' she asked, 'or are you doing the sensible thing and going back to the inn to rest?'

'I'm going back to the inn, but only because I have work to do there,' he told her tersely. 'I shall be at Stramore House later in the day.'

The air cleared after he had gone. Georgina inhaled deeply and gratefully. He exhausted her, just being with him exhausted her, but there wasn't time to sit and recuperate.

Robert was waiting when she reached the hotel. 'What on earth was all that about?' he wanted to know.

'Don't ask me,' said Georgina. 'He must think I'm his own personal property now I'm on his payroll.'

Robert frowned and she grimaced. 'Didn't I tell you? I no longer work for Valerie Arden—I'm his full-time interior designer. They conspired between them and he paid her a handsome sum so I can't really walk out on him—not yet! It might backlash on to Valerie, and I love that woman, I wouldn't want to hurt her.'

They spent the next hour going over some alterations he had made to the original design and after that he said he was going to the inn for his lunch. 'Come and join me,' he invited.

'I don't think that would be a very good idea,' she smiled. 'Leon's down there and I know what he'd have to say. I might go back to the cottage and have a sandwich, but I'm not really hungry.'

When Robert had gone Georgina wandered through the hotel, notepad and pencil in hand, a frown furrowing her brow, her thoughts now on the job she was supposed to be doing. Leon and Robert were already forgotten.

There was a vast difference from when she first came: very little was left of the debris that had littered the floors, most of the walls were plastered and the woodwork was finished. In fact some of the rooms were complete. It wouldn't be long now, she thought, before the whole project was ready for phase two—which was what she was here for.

One wing of the hotel still had some reconstruction work to do but that did not affect the bulk of the building. She stood watching one of the bricklayers, chewing the end of her pencil, admiring his skill.

He looked up and smiled and stopped what he was doing, putting down his trowel and straightening his back. 'It shouldn't be long now before it's finished. We're a bit behind schedule, I suppose. It's not affecting your job, is it?' He seemed to know exactly who she was.

'Not really,' confirmed Georgina.

'You're a lucky lass working for someone like Leon Alexander. Some people are ''B'''s to work for.'

'You like working for him, then?' It was a change to hear someone sing his praises after she had listened to Helen run him down for so long.

'Aye, that I do. He's a very fair man and he pays a good wage. He had every right to come down on us when the work was behind but he didn't.'

'Do you all feel the same about him?'

'Indeed we do. Everyone has a good word to say about him. I live in Stramore and there was a lot of talk when it was found out that this house had been sold. We were all worried about what was going to happen to it, whether it would affect the community. But what Leon's doing can only be good, it will bring money to the area. It will be real classy when it's finished according to what he's told us.'

Georgina found it interesting that Leon had talked to the builders in this vein. Most men in his position didn't bother to talk to the workers unless it was to give them instructions. She was suddenly seeing him in a very different light.

She continued to make notes, and before going back to the cottage she walked into the village to order some groceries. The provisions Leon had supplied were fast dwindling. 'How are you getting on up there?' asked

Mrs Johnson who owned the store. 'Not finding it too lonely?'

Georgina had never been in the shop before and was surprised that the woman knew all about her. 'Not at all.'

'It wouldn't suit a lot of young girls. But I expect Mr Alexander keeps you company?'

It looked as if the woman was the village gossip, thought Georgina with an inward smile. 'Actually, no, we have a strictly working relationship.'

'I saw you with that Mr Lacey. He's a nice boy too.'

'Yes, he is nice, isn't he?' confirmed Georgina handing over her list. 'I understand you can deliver?' The woman nodded. 'Thank you. I'll be in all afternoon. Good day, Mrs Johnson.' She walked quickly out of the shop before the woman could ask any further questions.

All afternoon Georgina worked at her drawing-board in the studio at the back of the cottage; time was forgotten, even Leon was forgotten. Rooms came to life in her mind's eye, sketches were pencilled, colours were decided and costings made. She felt very pleased with what she had accomplished.

She spent another whole day in her studio and, though she felt guilty that she was not keeping an eye on Leon as the doctor had suggested, she guessed that Sheena would be doing it for her. She preferred not to think of the two of them spending any time together, it was anathema to her, but it was inevitable so she had to accept it.

The following morning, wanting Leon's approval on the sketches and costings, she went in search of him. He was not at the hotel so she presumed he must be at the inn—perhaps even still resting! She spent a few minutes strolling along the lochside, inhaling appreciatively the fresh Highland air, listening to the chuckle of the water, watching a heron fishing. On the far bank the hills rose darkly green and somewhere hidden was Stramore House. It really was a perfect spot.

At the inn Sheena told her that Leon had gone to the airport.

'But he shouldn't be travelling in his condition,' frowned Georgina at once. 'Didn't you tell him that?'

'Believe me, I tried,' said Sheena. 'But when Leon makes up his mind no one can stop him.' The admiration shone out of her eyes and Georgina felt sickened.

'Where's he going?'

'He's not going anywhere, he's gone to meet someone. I've no idea who, he didn't say.' The telephone rang and Sheena broke off to answer and then handed it to Georgina. 'It's for you. Leon.'

Georgina frowned as she put the receiver to her ear. 'Yes, Leon?'

'What are you doing there?' he demanded harshly.

'Looking for you. I have some costings for your approval.'

'Then you can bring them to me. I'll meet you here at the hotel. No, we'd better make it the cottage, it's more private. And jump to it. I've wasted enough time already looking for you.'

Whatever he wanted to speak to her about must be urgent, thought Georgina as she hurried back up to the cottage, but she had the shock of her life when she walked in and saw Craig standing beside his uncle. Blond, handsome Craig. Not as tall as Leon but built like a rugby player, with laughing blue eyes and an irrepressible grin. He was the last person she had expected to see.

At this moment, though, he wasn't laughing. His shock was even greater than hers. Evidently Leon had said nothing to him about her.

'What's going on?' she ventured. 'What's Craig doing here?' She had a sudden feeling that something momentous was about to happen. Why had Craig come back from America? Why had Leon brought him up here? What had they got to say? It obviously involved her. Was Craig sticking to his story that she had been involved in his swindle? Had he spoilt things for her just when Leon was beginning to accept that she'd had nothing to do with it? In a fleeting second a thousand and one questions raced through her mind.

'I sent for him,' said Leon, indicating that she should sit down. The two men followed suit, Leon in the companion armchair to hers, Craig drawing up one of the wooden chairs from the table. 'Because of your continued insistence that you were innocent,' Leon carried on, 'I thought we should get together and thrash this thing out.' His bruise was still a violent purple; he looked as though he had been in a fight. Georgina felt sure he wasn't well enough to go chasing about.

'Thrash what out?' asked the younger man with a frown. 'What's going on?'

'I want you to tell me again, Craig,' said his uncle, 'why you stole that money.'

'But what's it got to do with Georgina?'

'Tell me!' insisted Leon.

Craig looked briefly at Georgina, his eyes puzzled, then said slowly, 'Because—because I thought I was in love. Because this girl meant everything to me and I wanted to buy her the earth. I didn't realise until afterwards that she was only interested in me because she thought I was rich. She knew you were my uncle. She knew I lived with you. She thought I had a share of your wealth.'

'And the name of this girl?' Leon's eyes were intent on his nephew.

'Dawn Riverson. Why is it so important? What's it got to do with Georgina?'

Leon paused before saying thickly, 'Because I thought Georgina was the girl in question.'

'*Georgina?*' echoed Craig. '*Georgina?* She's a girl in a million, as honest as the day is long. Georgina never wanted anything for herself, I had to force things on her. I wish she did love me, then none of this would have happened. I turned to Dawn on the rebound. I was a fool.'

Georgina studied her hands in her lap. She did not want to look at Leon. She was not the type to gloat because she had been proved right. In that moment she actually felt sorry for him.

'It seems I owe you an apology,' said Leon thickly.

She shrugged. 'It doesn't matter.'

'I've made a complete fool of myself.'

'Your reaction was understandable.'

'It matters a great deal. I dragged you up here because I wanted to hurt you. I thought you'd knowingly accepted gifts from Craig bought with stolen money. I've done you a great injustice.'

'Are you saying that she's not working here of her own free will?' asked Craig, a deep frown creasing his brow. 'Hell, Uncle, what have you done to her?' And to Georgina, 'You'd better come back with me. He's insane. He shouldn't have done this to you.'

'That will do, Craig,' said Leon firmly. 'What I did was entirely your fault. If you hadn't embezzled from the company then——'

'I know, I know,' cut in Craig. 'I'm sorry, I shouldn't have spoken like that, I was out of order. But I really have learned my lesson. Uncle Harry's a very hard man to work for. I realise just how kind you were to me and I'm going to pay you back, I promise, every penny of it. I'm working really hard—and I'm actually beginning to enjoy it. I think perhaps I wasn't cut out to work in an office after all. And I've met this stupendous girl there—she's wonderful. Once I've paid my debts to you I'm going to ask her to marry me.'

Leon looked in disbelief at his nephew. 'It doesn't take you long to change your affections, does it? I think you've a lot more growing up to do before you consider settling down.' He glanced at his watch. 'And if you want to catch that plane you'd better get moving.'

'If I'd known Georgina was here I wouldn't——'

'Craig!'

'OK, I'll go.' He stood up—as did Georgina—and he looked at her wryly. 'I'm sorry if my uncle's given you a hard time. I never thought that he'd jump to the wrong conclusion.'

Georgina smiled. 'At least it's all cleared up now. Are you heading straight back to the States?'

'No, I'm visiting a few friends.'

'Do you have to rush off? Can't you stay for a while?'

Craig glanced at Leon. 'I'm afraid not, it's all arranged.'

'So I won't see you again?'

He smiled. 'I wouldn't say that. Whenever I'm in England I'll most certainly look you up.'

'I'd like that,' she agreed. 'Perhaps I can drive you to the airport? Leon's not really fit to drive.'

Craig grinned. 'That eye's a beauty, isn't it? His car had a fight with a tree, so he told me.'

'Get going,' said Leon brusquely. 'And I'll do the driving, thank you, Georgina. I'll have a look at those costings later.'

When they had gone she sat down again. What a revealing few minutes those had been. It was hard to believe that Leon had sent for his nephew with the express purpose of clearing her name. She was happy about it, undoubtedly, but it seemed a crazy thing to do. He could have spoken to Craig on the phone and cleared it up that way just as easily.

Would it change things between them? Would that glimpse she had seen of some feeling for her become reality? Then she thought of Anita, and the bitterness with which he still regarded her, and knew it was not likely to happen. He had said he would never let any woman get close to him again—and he had meant every word.

It was almost five o'clock when Leon returned. He looked tired and his eyes were dull and she said at once, 'Leon, you should be resting, you shouldn't have come back here.'

'You have some figures you want me to go through?'

'Surely they can wait?'

'The sooner they're approved the sooner the wheels can be set in motion. Where are they?'

She silently handed them to him. 'Can I make you a cup of coffee or something?'

He smiled then. 'That would be nice. Thank you.'

They spent the next half-hour discussing the merits of relaxing pastel green rooms or warm honey gold. 'And are the bathrooms really going to cost this much?' he asked with a frown.

'If you want something classy and good, yes. If it's cheapness you're after, well——'

'Very well,' he cut in, 'point taken. What's the delivery?'

'Delivery's very good. Ten days. You won't better that.'

'Tell them to make it a week,' he said sharply, 'or we'll place the order elsewhere. But on the whole these are very good. You've made an excellent job of it so far, considering the difficulties you've experienced with no telephone and without an office on site. But that's all remedied. There are rooms now ready for us to move in.'

Georgina's eyes widened. So soon! She had not expected it so soon. Her heart clamoured. They were going to be living together! Well, almost together. In the same building. 'Are they furnished?' Was this what he had been doing the last couple of days?

'Yes, there is furniture.'

'I didn't realise things were so far advanced. When do you want me to move?'

'In the morning, I think. It's a little late now to be doing that sort of thing.'

'It will give me time to pack,' she agreed. 'Is the phone connected at the hotel now?'

'It is.'

'Will you be moving your office there as well?'

'But of course.'

So Sheena would be at the hotel! It was exactly what the girl wanted—and they would spend even more time together! Georgina felt sick with misery at the thought.

He stood up to go and she said, 'I'm glad we've cleared the air about Craig.'

He nodded. 'I did you an injustice.'

'You didn't have to go to all the trouble of fetching him back here.'

'There was a reason.'

Georgina waited but when it was not forthcoming she said. 'Anyway, I'm glad.' And she smiled, a warm, friendly smile, hoping that it would tell him that she wanted them to be friends.

But all he did was nod gravely and walk towards the door. 'I'll see you in the morning.'

'Are you in pain, Leon?' Georgina posed the question anxiously. There wasn't the easiness between them that she had expected.

'My head hurts, yes. I plan to have a long, lazy evening. Is that to your approval?'

'Indeed it is. You shouldn't have done all that driving today. You should be taking things easy.'

'One would think you really cared.'

His tone was so full of sarcasm that Georgina knew she dared not press home the fact that she did. He wouldn't believe her in any case.

When he had gone the cottage felt empty. He always had this effect on it. He filled it with his presence, gave it an added dimension, and now she was alone it had all gone. She was surrounded by four square walls, cold brick walls, and she wrapped her arms around herself and sat in the chair he had vacated.

She would be leaving this cottage and in one way she was sad, yet in another she rejoiced at the thought of being nearer to Leon. Would things be different now that he no longer had any reason to harass her, now that Craig was no longer a stumbling-block between them?

That night, after packing her few belongings, she slept easily and when Leon came to collect her a little before nine she was ready. Into his car went her drawing materials and notebooks, swatches of fabric and piles of brochures, her own suitcase and plastic carrier bags filled with shoes and odds and ends.

She would miss this little cottage, she thought, taking a last look around. For all its lack of amenities she had enjoyed living here, far more than Leon had ever envisaged.

The rooms that they were going to use were at the back of the house, rooms which would eventually be the living quarters for some of the staff, rooms that had not needed very much doing to them. They had been freshly wallpapered and painted and there was a bathroom with a shower. There was a lounge, a kitchen and two bedrooms, each adequately furnished, though not with the sort of pieces she would have chosen herself.

'If you'll follow me,' said Leon, 'I'll show you where you're going to work.'

Upstairs again, right to the very top. The room had a skylight as well as two windows. It was a very large room. At one end stood a large antique desk, a drawing-board and a filing cabinet, and a telephone. In fact everything she would need. There were two more desks at the other end of the room, with the usual complement of phones and files, and pens and pencils. She frowned.

'We're all working up here,' he said, 'until the new office is ready. Sheena should be here any minute.'

Some of Georgina's pleasure faded. She had not expected this. She would not have objected to sharing with Leon, but Sheena too? Sheena's dog-like devotion to Leon was more than she could stand.

He read her face all too clearly. 'You don't like the idea?'

'Not really,' she answered crisply.

'Is it Sheena or me you object to?'

Georgina lifted her shoulders. 'I shall find it difficult to concentrate.'

'But I'm sure you'll manage.' He looked at her long and hard, his concentration broken by a crashing sound from somewhere in the depths of the house. He ran out of the room, stopping only to say, 'You'd best phone an order for groceries through to the village shop. But don't worry about cooking a meal tonight; we're eating out.'

Don't worry about cooking a meal! Was that what she was expected to do? Was she supposed to clean and cook and look after him? Her temper rose but at that moment Sheena entered the room. 'What's going on? I met Leon tearing downstairs, and I heard this most terrible noise.'

Georgina shrugged. 'He's gone to find out. I don't expect it's much, though. The builders are always doing something.'

It was over an hour before Leon came back, and when he did so his face was grave.

'What's happened?' asked Georgina at once. She had not dreamt it was anything serious.

'A ceiling collapsed and hurt one of the men. He's been taken to hospital. He's in a critical condition but we don't know yet the full extent of his injuries.'

'How did it happen?'

'Because some damn fool knocked down a wall without first jacking up the ceiling. And the ironic part is that the wall should never have come down in the first place.'

'I don't understand.' Georgina's frown deepened. 'Robert's plans are perfectly clear.'

'He's a new lad, an apprentice, and he went ahead without asking anyone.'

And now everything would be delayed. She knew it was on his mind even though he did not put his thoughts into actual words. 'I'm sorry, Leon.'

'Dinner's off tonight,' he said roughly. 'We'll eat here. Robert's coming. We're going over the plans to see if we can accommodate this disaster without too much rebuilding.'

CHAPTER SEVEN

LEON and Robert ate their meal without even seeming to taste it. They were absorbed completely in discussions about the hotel and Georgina was ignored.

'Coffee, gentlemen?' Her question fell on deaf ears so she made it anyway and then went up to the studio.

It was ten o'clock and still light, and she settled down to do some work and was so totally engrossed that she did not hear Robert go or Leon come upstairs.

'So there you are,' he said. 'I thought you'd gone to bed.'

She looked up and saw the lines of strain on his face and felt full of compassion for him. He could do without troubles of this sort while his head was so bad. 'Have you worked things out?'

'I think so. Robert sends a message.' His tone was clipped, almost as though he did not want to pass it on. 'He wants to take you out to dinner tomorrow night.'

Georgina smiled. 'How nice. Did he say what time he'll pick me up?' She would have preferred to go with Leon. It was a shame tonight had been cancelled. She had been looking forward to it.

Leon eyed her coldly. 'I told him you're far too busy. That it's unlikely you'll have any free time for a while yet.'

'You did what?' She shot to her feet, her green eyes filled with sudden anger. 'How dare you? I have no intention of working all hours to please you.'

'You'll do what I say.' His tone was firm and brooked no argument.

'I work for you, Mr Alexander, I now live with you—unfortunately, it would seem—but you don't own me. If I want to go out with Robert then I will and you won't stop me.'

He grinned, his shark's grin that held no pleasure. 'You underestimate me, Georgina.'

'And you, you callous brute, underestimate me. I am my own woman. I do what I want to do.'

Still he smiled. 'Has anyone ever told you how beautiful you are when you're angry?'

'No one's ever made me as angry as you,' she spat.

'Meaning it's a clash of personalities?'

'Exactly. We're never, ever likely to get on. If it weren't that I enjoyed the challenge of this job I wouldn't stay here.'

'And that's the only thing that's keeping you?' His eyes narrowed and it seemed as though her answer was important to him.

'Yes,' she lied bravely. She could not tell him that she had stayed on because of his injury, or that she was now hoping their relationship might develop because the truth had come out about Craig.

'Not the fact that you know you won't find another job?'

'If I did leave here,' she told him coldly, 'I'd set up on my own. I know I'm not quite ready for it but I've no doubt I'd manage.'

A flicker of admiration showed on his face, gone instantly. She might even have imagined it.

'If you'll excuse me,' she said, 'I'm going to make myself a drink and then I'm going to bed. Goodnight.' Her eyes averted, as if by not looking at him she could ignore his suffocating power, Georgina walked determinedly towards the door. Her skin prickled as she moved within a few inches of him; she felt devastating vibrations, every nerve taut.

'No goodnight kiss?'

The softness of his tone was deceptive, and it did not fool her for one second. One step and he was standing in front of her, a firm finger lifting her chin, compelling her to look at him.

An impossible heat invaded her body, her heart fluttered like a captive bird, but she kept all emotion out of her eyes, looking at him coldly and aloofly. 'Please let me pass.'

'Not until you've kissed me goodnight.'

Georgina wanted his kiss, she wanted it very much, but she knew where such a kiss could lead. And what was the point when Leon had no more interest in her than he'd had in any other girl he'd dated since the Anita affair? She was a game to him, that was all. Sheena was a game to him. When he'd said that he never intended falling in love again he had meant every word. He would let no girl get close.

At this moment, though, he was still waiting for her kiss. She smiled softly and, lifting her face, kissed him perfunctorily on his cheek, and before his arms could possess her she twisted quickly and successfully away. She saw the swift stab of annoyance in his eyes and smiled to herself as she headed downstairs. He had expected more, he had wanted more. Was this how to get through to him?

She made herself a cup of hot drinking chocolate and took it to bed, sitting up and sipping it as she thought about Leon. She felt far too vulnerable here in this house with him in the quiet of the night. What did the workmen think about the arrangement? Did they know? Was there talk?

Not that it worried her. So long as her own conscience was clear it was all that mattered.

She put her mug down on the floor and snuggled beneath the quilt, closing her eyes, praying that sleep would claim her quickly, but not surprised when it didn't. How could she sleep in these circumstances? How could she sleep when Leon was in the next room? How was she ever going to get a good night's sleep again while they were here?

Somewhere an owl hooted and there were the usual creaks of a house settling down for the night. Each one made her start, wondering whether it was Leon, whether he too was having difficulty in sleeping. Wondering, even, whether he would come to her room. The thought sent a shiver down her spine, not fear, not cold, but excitement. Despite everything that had happened he was by far the most interesting man she had ever met. He intrigued her, he excited her, and she was more than halfway towards falling in love with him!

It was a startling discovery and she pushed it away again quickly. In love? With Leon? What nonsense! No man had ever treated her so badly as he had. Why should she fall in love with him?

Eventually, after many hours spent tossing and turning, sleep came to her but she woke early, not much after five, and already it was a clear blue day. She would go for a walk, she decided; she needed to clear her head of all the thoughts muddling through it.

She pulled on a skirt and thin cotton sweater. The air was cool at this hour, the sun without any real warmth. The loch below was still and silent—and tempted her with its serenity.

Beyond the village was a tiny wooden pier with several rowing boats and fishing boats tied on either side. An old man with a crinkled, leathery face sat on one of the boats, smoking a pipe, completely at peace with the world.

'Good morning,' said Georgina cheerfully, and it seemed sacrilege to shatter the silence.

The old man evidently thought so too because he was a long time in answering. It was almost as though he did not want her there.

'Are any of these boats for hire?' she asked next.

He scratched his chin with the mouthpiece of his pipe. 'Aye, lassie, if you come back about ten.'

'I'll be working then,' she said, her disappointment showing. 'I wanted to get out there now and find myself some peace.'

A wiry grey eyebrow rose. 'Peace? A young lass like you? Are you having some kind of troubles?'

Georgina shrugged and smiled wryly. 'Not really, I suppose. But the loch looked so tempting from up there.'

'You're up at the House, isn't that right? With Mr Alexander? Moved out of your wee cottage? He's turning it into a hotel, I believe. It's going to spoil Stramore. Too many holidaymakers. They'll want pleasure boats on the loch. No more peace then. What is your relationship with Mr Alexander?'

His direct question made Georgina smile. News had certainly travelled fast. 'He's my employer. I'm an interior designer.'

'So why are you living with him?'

'Because...' This was going to be a difficult question to answer. 'Because we're working closely together on this project, and the cottage wasn't really suitable.'

'I see, and is it the man himself you're running away from this early in the morning?'

For someone who resented his peace being disrupted he was asking an awful lot of questions. Were all the villagers as curious? she wondered. And was she running away from Leon?

The answer to that question had to be yes. Not Leon as a person but the situation he had created. Georgina was not sure that she could continue to live with him if, after only one night, she was on edge. But she smiled at the old man and shook her head. 'Of course not. I was awake early and it was such a beautiful morning that I wanted to enjoy it.'

'You can take my boat if you like. You can row, I take it?'

'Oh, yes. I have three brothers and I was always determined to do whatever they did. I've been rowing lots of times.'

He nodded his head and sucked on his pipe. 'Aye, then, I guess it will be all right.' Slowly he stood up and equally as slowly his gnarled fingers untied the old boat. He held it steady while she got in and positioned her oars in the rowlocks, then he pushed her gently away from the pier.

'I'll be back in an hour,' she said gaily. 'Thank you very much. I appreciate it.'

The movement of the boat disturbed the oil-smooth surface of the water. She pulled in long, effortless strokes, soon developing a steady rhythm, watching the shingle shore of the loch getting further and further away. The old man was talking to someone else now. Someone else who had risen early to enjoy the soft morning air of the Highlands.

After ten minutes she was near the island. Stramore Island, it was called. No one was allowed to go on it, she had discovered, as it was used entirely as a nature reserve. She rowed round to the other side and then stopped, letting the boat sit silently in the water, listening to the faint rustlings and squawkings going on out of sight. A red-throated diver, disturbed out of his sleep, paddled closer to look at her, and then dived beneath the water for his breakfast, coming up a few seconds later with a small silver fish which slid down his throat in a couple of swallows.

She moved on, reaching the other shore now, its wooded slopes rising high above her. Somewhere up there was Leon, hopefully still fast asleep. She craned her neck, trying to see the house—and the next second the boat hit a rock half buried in the shallows.

Georgina stifled a curse at her own stupidity in not looking where she was going and quickly pushed herself back into deeper waters.

Glancing at her watch, she was amazed to see how long she had been out. It was time to head back. Humming happily to herself, she pulled on the oars, her actions automatic, allowing her thoughts to return to Leon.

It would be fun trying to get through to him—if fun was the right word—though she would have to be very careful how she went about it. She dared not let him guess that she harboured any feelings for him. On the other hand, if Robert wanted to take her out she would go, let Leon say what he liked. She needed other people to talk to—*and why were her feet getting wet*?

When she looked down Georgina saw to her horror that water was seeping into the bottom of the boat. For the first time she noticed that the floor was a bit rotten and she must have helped it on its way when she hit the rock.

She was a strong swimmer so wasn't worried about drowning, but the thought of sinking the old man's boat did bother her. And all because she had wanted to get away from Leon!

She felt for the hole, wondering if she could plug it with something, but even as her fingers touched it some more of the wood crumbled away and the water came in even faster.

Georgina began to row quickly now, hoping she might reach the other shore before the boat filled with water but it gurgled in more quickly still so she abandoned that attempt and tried to scoop it out with her hands. A futile effort. She sat there for a few seconds longer before taking the only course left open to her.

The water was cold and took her breath away and it was much further than she had thought. About a hundred yards from the shore she saw the old man standing watching her, and his companion looked like Leon. A few yards closer she saw that it was indeed him and her spirits sank. The last thing she wanted was Leon seeing her like this.

As soon as her feet touched the bottom she stood up and waded the rest of the way. She had taken off her shoes and skirt before diving into the water and the pebbles hurt her feet and she kept stumbling and the old man's face was a picture of concern. 'What happened? I knew the old boat was on its last legs, but I never dreamt it would let you down.'

Leon on the other hand was grinning. 'Have you enjoyed your morning's swim, Georgina?'

She gasped for air, her teeth chattering, hardly able to keep a limb still. 'I could have drowned for all you care.'

'From what I could see there was no fear of that. You're an excellent swimmer. Here, let me help you to the road.'

'No, thanks.' She snatched her arm away from him. And to the old man she said, 'I'm sorry about your boat,

I really am. I accidentally holed the bottom. I'm afraid
it sank.'

He shrugged. 'It wasn't worth much, it doesn't matter
so long as you're all right?'

Georgina suddenly realised that her thin cotton jumper
had turned transparent in the water. Her nipples were
erect and Leon was studying them as she spoke to the
other man.

'I'll come and see you again,' she said. 'I'd like to
compensate you in some way. I must get back now, I'm
freezing.'

'I have my car,' said Leon abruptly. He opened the
door for her, fetched a blanket out of his boot and
draped it over the seat, and when she was inside wrapped
it around her.

'You don't have to fuss,' she said irritably, even though
at the same time she felt the full impact of his nearness.

'I don't want you catching cold.'

'Because you're afraid I might be too sick to work?
Or because you might be forced to look after me now
that we're living together? Or perhaps a mixture of
both?' she finished, embarrassment making her tone
sharp. What a fool to let herself get into such a situation.

He slid in the other side and started the engine. 'Would
you believe me if I said it was none of those things, that
I was just thinking of you?'

If only that were true! But she knew exactly the way
he thought about her—and it definitely wasn't on a
caring, personal level. 'No, I wouldn't,' she retorted.

His lips wry, he said, 'Never mind; tell me how you
managed to sink the boat. I watched you row away, you
looked as though you were very experienced. I must
admit, Georgina, that you continually surprise me.'

'I'm sorry if I woke you when I left the house,' she said, deliberately ignoring his question, 'but you didn't have to come after me.'

'I thought you were running away.'

Her eyes widened. 'Without taking any of my clothes? Why did you think that?'

'You're not happy with me, are you, Georgina?'

She shrugged. 'Sometimes I am, sometimes I'm not. It depends how you treat me.'

'You don't like to think that you're a prisoner here?'

'Most certainly not. And if I were really determined I would go, threats or no threats, and you wouldn't be able to stop me.'

He smiled. 'I admire your fighting spirit, Georgina, but you haven't answered my earlier question.'

'And I don't intend to.'

'Were you perhaps not looking where you were going for some reason?'

It was almost as though he knew, and yet how could he have seen her from that distance? 'My concentration was temporarily broken,' she admitted.

The car drew to a halt outside the house and Georgina grabbed the door-handle with one hand and the blanket with the other, but it was wrapped so tightly around her legs that she was unable to move.

Leon came round and picked her up as though she were a baby, carrying her into the house despite her demands that he put her down, setting her to her feet, whipping the blanket away from her as he did so. She was thankful it was too early for the workmen to have arrived. It would have been too embarrassing by far to have them see her in this condition.

'You're totally irresistible in that get-up.' His eyes were narrowed and assessing, his mouth hovering on the verge of a smile. 'It's a wonder you didn't give that man out there a heart attack.'

'Very funny,' glared Georgina. Her hair looked much darker than its usual light chestnut colour and was plastered close to her head instead of bouncing in a riot of uncontrollable waves.

'Is that how you look when you come out of the bath?' He touched a wet curl, letting it sit on his finger, while the back of his hand brushed her cheek. 'You're shivering,' he observed. 'Go and take a shower and get into some dry clothes before you catch cold.'

Georgina turned and ran up the stairs. She could feel his eyes on her and was acutely conscious of her state of semi-nudity. She wasn't cold, she felt on fire—and all because he had held her in his arms! The power this man had over her was astonishing.

She turned the shower on full and stood beneath its invigorating jets, closing her eyes and letting it rain down over her for several minutes. She felt more conscious of her body than ever before and knew it was because of the way Leon had looked at her when she came out of the loch. His eyes had feasted on her, seeing her femininity, knowing that she was aware of him watching her, knowing that she was affected by it.

Disgusted with herself, Georgina turned off the water and towelled herself thoroughly dry. Wrapped in the towel, she returned to her bedroom and quickly dressed, and as she put on her watch she noticed that it was still only twenty past seven. She could not believe that so much had happened before the day had even begun.

In the kitchen she filled the kettle and switched it on. Would Leon expect her to cook his breakfast, and where was he anyway? As if aware of the line her thoughts were taking he suddenly appeared. 'Would you like some toast?' she asked, not daring to look at him as she dropped two slices of bread into the toaster. It was hard when really all she wanted to do was turn around and feast her eyes on him.

'Please.' He sat down at the kitchen table, watching her, sending her temperature soaring, his eyes never off her. 'How are you feeling? No after-effects?'

She glanced at him then, and her breath caught in her throat at the intensity of his gaze. 'I'm fine.'

'Good.'

That was all he said and yet she sensed there was a whole depth of meaning behind the word. He actually cared. He did not want her catching cold. It was unbelievable.

They sat together and ate their toast and drank their coffee. A cosy, domestic scene, thought Georgina, except that there was nothing cosy about their relationship. It was filled with tension, at least on her part. This was their first day together and she felt like this! What was it going to be like after a week, a month? Would it be an impossible situation? Would she find it unbearable? Why had she agreed? Why hadn't she insisted on staying at the cottage?

Thankfully he did not linger over his meal. The workmen arrived at eight and he went down to make sure everything was going according to plan. Georgina washed up and then shut herself away in the studio.

Robert came up to see her halfway through the morning. 'Did Leon pass on my message?'

Georgina smiled. 'Begrudgingly, yes.'

'You will come out with me?'

'Of course. It's very kind of you to ask. And very brave after the way Leon spoke to you.'

Robert shrugged. 'Leon's bark is worse than his bite. He can't really stop us seeing each other.' He came closer to her desk and stood looking down at her. 'I'm not sure that I like you living here with him. Is it necessary? I thought the cottage was ideal.'

Georgina shrugged. 'It was Leon's idea. I didn't have any choice.'

'Are you getting on any better?'

Georgina shrugged. 'We have our ups and downs, although I can't see us ever getting really close. He's still not changed his mind about girls in general. We're a commodity to be used and discarded.'

Georgina did not realise how bitter she sounded until Robert said sadly, 'So you're still in love with him?'

'In love?' she echoed. 'I've never told you I was actually in love with Leon.'

'No, but it's there on your face when you talk about him, and in your eyes when you look at him.'

'Oh, goodness, is it really?' she asked, appalled. 'Do I give myself away that much?'

'Don't panic, Georgina,' he smiled. 'It's visible only to me—because I love you myself.'

She grimaced. 'Oh, Robert, I'm so sorry.'

'Don't be. I know I'll never be number one where you're concerned. But I'm prepared to settle for the odd date—and I shall always hope.'

'You're a man in a million, Robert. I wish I did love you.' She stood up and faced him and he put his hands on her shoulders. 'I guess we're both destined to love someone who doesn't love us in return.' His lips twisted. 'At least we have a bond.'

She nodded. 'Life's very unfair, don't you think?'

'Very,' he confirmed and, bending, he kissed her lightly on the forehead. 'At least I have tonight to look forward to.'

They both looked up when the door swung open. Leon stopped abruptly in his tracks when he saw them, his eyes darkening. 'Forgive me if I'm interrupting.' His voice was at its most sarcastic. 'But there's a rep here to see you, Georgina—if you can possibly spare the time.'

The man was behind him and Robert moved quickly away. 'I'll pick you up at about eight, Gina?'

She nodded, avoiding Leon's eyes, looking straight at the man who had come to see her.

'Mike Gould, Ross Carpets,' he announced.

It was early afternoon when Georgina began to sneeze, and by teatime her nose and eyes were streaming and she ached in every limb. She had eaten a sandwich for her lunch, expecting Leon to come and confront her, relieved when there was no sign of him. Now, when he came up to their rooms, he took one look at her and ordered her to bed.

'It's just a bit of a cold,' she demurred. 'I can't go to bed, I'm meeting Robert.'

'You're not going out with Robert or anyone else tonight,' he said firmly. 'It looks to me as though you've caught a chill. Taking that boat out was a crazy thing to do—you must have known it was rotten. Bob admitted to me that it was ready for the scrap-heap.'

'He didn't tell me that,' she frowned.

'He said you seemed anxious to get out on the loch, that you needed peace. Was that because of me? Is it going to be too much for you, us living together?'

Before she could answer Georgina sneezed again and dabbed her handkerchief to her streaming eyes.

'Get to bed,' said Leon firmly. 'I'll bring you some hot milk and aspirin.'

And Georgina felt so ill that she obeyed. She took off her clothes and crawled beneath the quilt. She felt on fire and yet at the same time was shivering.

Leon came in with the milk and tablets, standing over her while she swallowed them. He put a hand to her brow and frowned. 'You're burning up. Maybe I should send for the doctor?'

It was a sign of Georgina's condition that she felt no response to Leon's touch, not a missed heartbeat or even the skipping of a pulse. 'Just let me sleep, I'll be all right,' she said, handing him back the empty glass and curling up into a ball beneath the covers.

He looked doubtful and she knew he stood there for a minute after she closed her eyes, but he moved away finally.

After that sleep claimed her, but she woke many times, sweating, tossing and turning, aching in every limb, feeling a cool face-cloth wiping the perspiration from her brow but too weak to wonder who was doing it.

Sometimes Leon was in the room with her, sitting beside the bed, looking at her with such tenderness and concern that she knew it had to be a dream, a hallucination.

Time had no meaning but finally she awoke and felt a little better, though not much. Through the window she could see the tops of the Scots pines bowing in the breeze, and a blue sky shadowed with cumulus clouds.

She ought to get up, she thought, but when she swung her legs over the edge of the bed they would not support her weight. They felt as though every bone had been taken out and replaced with cotton wool.

Leon came into the room and ordered her immediately back to bed.

'But I'm feeling much better,' she protested.

'You don't look it. Are you hungry? I've some broth on the stove.'

'Have you made it?' It was strange how unlikely the thought of Leon cooking was.

'I have.'

'For me?'

'You need something nourishing.'

'You sound like my mother.'

'Do I?' His lips quirked. 'I don't feel maternal where you're concerned.' He straightened the quilt and looked close into her eyes. 'Not one little bit.'

Georgina could smell his own particular brand of maleness and was swamped with a warmth that now had nothing to do with her illness. She tried to sink back on the pillows away from him but there was no escape. 'What time is it?' she asked, in an attempt to distract him.

'Three o'clock.'

She frowned. 'Thursday?'

'That's right.'

'I've slept almost twenty-four hours!'

'Slept is hardly the right word. You've been delirious a lot of the time. It's more than just a chill, you've got flu. Several of the workmen are off with it.'

Georgina frowned. 'If I've got flu you shouldn't be nursing me—you'll catch it too.'

'No, I won't, I was vaccinated against it a few weeks ago. Stay there now and I'll fetch your broth.'

Such was the power of the man that the room seemed empty when he had gone and Georgina closed her eyes to reflect on her feelings for him. Was Robert right, was she truly in love with Leon? Was that why she had put up with his treatment of her? And would he ever return her love? Would he get over the way Anita had treated him? Would he learn to trust again?

She had no way of knowing the answer to these questions and was still puzzling over them when he returned. The tray which he laid on her bed held a china soup-cup full of steaming broth, a bread roll, a napkin, and, to her surprise, a blush-pink carnation in a tiny glass vase.

Georgina raised an eyebrow. 'You've gone to all this trouble for me?'

'I'm not completely inhuman when someone's ill.'

'Perhaps I should be ill all the time?'

A reproving eyebrow rose and he let the comment pass. 'Eat your broth while it's hot.'

It was full of pieces of tender lamb and a mixture of fresh vegetables and Georgina took a spoonful. It was delicious but she wasn't really hungry. 'Where did you learn to cook like this?'

'When a man lives alone he has no choice. I enjoy it.'

'You surprise me. I never envisaged you doing anything like this. Don't you have a housekeeper?'

'Yes, but I still think a man should be able to fend for himself if necessary.'

She managed another spoonful, even breaking off a piece of bread and dipping it into the tasty broth.

He watched as she popped it into her mouth and she felt herself grow warm again under his surveillance. A mischievous smile curved her lips. 'Now I know you're so clever we can share the cooking.'

'I don't think so, Georgina.'

'You mean you're a male chauvinist?'

'Some people might say that.' His lips quirked as he spoke.

'Is that why you've never found yourself another girl to settle down with? Do you domineer them too much?'

His face darkened with each question that she asked and Georgina knew she ought to shut up but some devil drove her on. 'Do they leave you when they find out what you're like?'

'Shut up, Georgina, and eat your broth.' There was a threatening darkness to his eyes and a caustic tone to his voice.

She took another sip but it was all getting too much for her. Her brief flare of energy had gone, weariness overcame her and she wanted no more of the broth he had gone to all the trouble to make. She rested the spoon in the dish. 'I'm sorry, Leon, I can't eat any more. I'm not hungry.'

The blaze in his eyes faded as he picked up the spoon himself and tried to cajole her, tried to feed her as one did a child. 'Georgina.' His arm came about her shoulders. 'You really must eat, you're doing yourself no good.'

It felt good to be held by him. Leon in this mood was the most perfect man she had ever met and silently she prayed that he might relax his rigid views and allow her to creep into his life.

With that thought she took two more mouthfuls, then she turned her head away, 'I'm tired, Leon, I've had enough. I want to rest.'

With a displeased twist to his mouth he lifted the tray and set it to one side. But he seemed in no hurry to leave. He sat beside the bed and watched her, straightening the quilt as she curled back down beneath it, smoothing a stray strand of hair from her face, and she wondered how many hours he had sat and watched her like this while she slept. The thought brought a warm flush of colour to her cheeks.

She closed her eyes but was too aware of him to sleep. Her body still ached, her head felt muzzy, but her feelings for Leon were stronger—and getting stronger all the time! What would have happened to her if she were still in the cottage? Would Leon have moved in and looked after her there?

The thought brought a faint smile to her lips and she opened her eyes and looked at him, disturbing an unusual tenderness in his eyes, a softness to his expression. It was gone in an instant, replaced by carefully assumed nonchalance, but she knew she had not imagined it and the thought made her feel good.

'I have to go out, Georgina. Will you be all right?'

Disappointment crept in. This was a rare moment of togetherness that she did not want to end. 'Where are you going?' It was not a question one usually asked Leon Alexander, but she felt that under the circumstances she had every right.

'I'm going to see young Ferguson. He's still on the critical list.'

Georgina had forgotten about the accident yesterday, or was it the day before? Her mind felt too muddled to work it out. 'Oh, of course. You must be very worried about him.' She knew that if anything happened to the boy Leon would feel personally responsible. She held out her hand, softening her tone. 'I'm sure he'll recover, Leon, and you don't have to worry about me; stay as long as you like.'

He took her hand and squeezed it tightly. 'But I do worry, Georgina; you've become a part of my life. I can't imagine it now without you.'

CHAPTER EIGHT

LEON'S words stayed with Georgina for a long time. *He could not imagine life without her!* In what respect? As a friend? An employee? A colleague? A lover? A wife? By the time her thoughts had got to this stage her heart was thumping fit to burst and she was impatient to get well again.

She noticed a marked difference in their relationship. Her illness brought them closer together, Leon's hours of tending her every need driving away his bitterness and distrust, and she thought there was a very real chance now of something developing between them. The boy had come off the critical list as well so there was nothing at all for him to worry about.

He walked into her room one day with a large bouquet of pink roses and her cheeks glowed as she sat up in bed to receive them. 'Leon, they're beautiful, thank you.' She inhaled their gentle perfume appreciatively. It was the first time a man had ever given her flowers. 'They're just what I need to brighten the room up. How thoughtful of you.'

'They're not from me,' he announced abruptly.

She looked at him and frowned and wondered why she had not noticed the tightness of his jaw. 'Then who's sent them?'

'There's a card. Why don't you read it?'

She picked up the envelope and slid out the tiny white rectangle.

Please get well soon,
Love, Robert.

She swallowed. 'They're from Robert.'

'Naturally,' he drawled. 'He sends his love, does he? He was quite disturbed to hear you were ill. I had a hell of a job keeping him away.'

Georgina frowned. 'I thought it was because he didn't want to catch my flu?'

'I told him it would be a strong possibility and that he had a duty to other people, if not himself, to avoid it if he could.'

To a certain degree Georgina agreed with him, but that didn't give him the right to take it upon himself to stop Robert seeing her. 'I wondered why he hadn't been, or even sent a message. Did you withhold those too?' Her tone was suddenly suspicious.

'You know how I feel about Robert.'

'And I know that this is a free country. You're a swine, Leon.' All the warm, happy feelings had gone.

His brows lifted, his mouth twisted mockingly. 'It sounds as though you're getting better.'

'I am, and I have you to thank for that, I know, but when I'm fully recovered I intend going out with Robert, and you won't stop me.'

Georgina wished he hadn't made her say that. It sounded as though she was more interested in Robert than him. Why did this have to happen now, just when things were getting better between them?

Her recovery took several more days and even when she started back to work she tired easily. There was still an atmosphere between her and Leon—it was almost as though he was jealous of Robert and yet she did not see why that should be.

The hotel office was now ready and he and Sheena had moved down there, much to her relief. She had not looked forward to working in the same room. Sheena seemed to have an extra glow about her these days and it was not difficult to guess why. Whenever Georgina needed to check something with Leon they were always closeted together.

On the second day she was back in the studio Robert came to see her. 'So the invalid has returned,' he said, a warm smile on his lips. 'How are you feeling?'

'Still a little groggy,' she admitted. 'I don't think I've ever been so ill. Thank you for the flowers, they were lovely.'

'You've lost weight. Are you sure you're fit enough for work?'

She nodded. 'Oh, yes. I've had enough sitting around doing nothing.'

'Leon wouldn't let me come to see you.' Robert looked disgruntled at the thought.

'So he said,' confirmed Georgina wryly. 'In fact I was rather cross with him about it.'

'He had a point,' he admitted grudgingly, 'but I think it was rather more personal than because he didn't want me catching the flu. He still doesn't approve of my seeing you, does he?'

Georgina shook her head.

'And yet he's more than friendly with Sheena, so why should it bother him?'

'Don't ask me,' said Georgina, her lips compressed. She did not need Robert telling her how much time they spent together.

'So how about letting me take you out for that dinner tonight? You definitely need cheering up.'

'I'd love to, Robert,' she said without hesitation.

He looked pleased. 'I'll pick you up at eight.'

Leon's face hardened when she told him she was going out with Robert, his disapproval clear by the blazing fury in his eyes. If he had said, Cancel your date with Robert, I'll take you out myself, she would have accepted, eagerly, but there was nothing except censure, and it hurt, even more than she cared to admit.

Even so, as she got ready for her dinner date she could not help wishing it were Leon she was going out with. She would have been buoyed up with excitement by now instead of feeling nothing but mediocre pleasure.

Georgina was ready and waiting long before Robert rang the bell. 'Don't wait up for me, Leon,' she said with enforced gaiety as she left the room. She missed his deep frown of annoyance.

Although she was upset by Leon's attitude she was determined not to let thoughts of him spoil their evening. She was going to enjoy every minute.

In his car Robert smiled at her warmly. 'I'm glad you're here.'

She returned his smile and nodded.

'Did Leon have anything to say?'

'Not a word.'

His brows rose in surprise.

'But he wasn't pleased, I could tell.'

'I'm sorry he's giving you a hard time again.'

'It's not your fault,' she said at once. 'Why shouldn't you ask me out? Why should we let Leon dictate? He's a swine. I sometimes think I hate him.'

Robert's lips twisted. 'He's a difficult man to understand, I've always known that. His life hasn't been easy what with his parents splitting up, bringing up young Craig, and then all that trouble with Anita. He's had a lot to contend with. It's made him bitter.'

'But he's not always,' argued Georgina. 'I've seen him when he's different, when he's human, when he's like everyone else.'

'But it isn't often enough?'

'No,' she admitted sadly.

Robert sighed. 'Life never goes the way we want it to, Gina. What we have to do is make the best of what we've got. And for tonight I've got you!' He grinned as he said it and Georgina realised it would be unfair to burden him with her problems for the rest of the evening.

She grinned back. 'You're right, Robert. Let's enjoy ourselves.'

They went to the same little restaurant overlooking the loch that he had taken her to before and Georgina was able to relax as she never could with Leon. Why couldn't she love Robert? she asked herself sadly. There would be no problems then.

When they came out she saw the old man ambling slowly along the shore, his pipe stuck firmly in his mouth. 'Excuse me a minute,' she said to Robert, and ran across to speak to him.

His leathery face creased into a smile when he saw her. 'I'm sorry I've not been to see you before,' she said at once, 'but I've had the flu and I've only just got over it.'

'Aye, Mr Alexander told me. You still look a wee bit pale.'

Leon had spoken to him about her? She found that surprising. 'About your boat,' she went on. 'I must give you something. I feel really awful about it.'

'Och, away with you, it wasn't worth a thing. I'm the one who's feeling guilty. You could have drowned.'

'I wouldn't have taken the boat out if I couldn't swim.' she said. 'Thank you for being so understanding. I'm afraid I can't stay and talk now—I'm with a friend. Perhaps I'll see you around some time?'

'I'll look forward to that, lassie,' he smiled. 'I don't have much company these days except my own.'

Which he seemed to enjoy! She rejoined Robert and he took her home. 'Shall I come up with you?' he asked, concerned that Leon might vent his anger on her yet again.

Georgina shook her head and smiled. 'You're worrying for nothing. Leon can't say or do anything. I'm a free agent.'

But it was with caution that she opened the door and crept up to their rooms. All was silent and in darkness. Relief flooded through her. He must have gone out or to bed. But in her bedroom she got the shock of her life when she snapped on the light and found Leon sitting on the edge of her bed.

'How dare you come in here?' she cried at once, green eyes flashing.

'How did your evening go?' He stood up and looked at her, his face all hard, uncompromising lines. The bruise was more yellow than purple now, but it still looked fearsome.

'As if you care,' she snapped.

'Did you enjoy it?'

'Of course I did. Robert's good company.'

'Meaning I'm not?'

'Not when you're in this mood,' she thrust. 'I really don't know what you've got against Robert.'

'I don't like to think of you in any other man's arms.'

Her brows rose at that unexpected statement. 'Why should it matter to you?'

'Because you're my property.'

'*Your* property!' she echoed incredulously. 'What are you talking about?'

He took a step towards her, his eyes still intent on hers. 'One day, Georgina, I intend to own you completely.'

A *frisson* of fear ran through her, followed closely by other feelings she was afraid to reveal. Deep, deep, highly personal feelings, sensual feelings. With a cry of anger she swung away, only to have his fingers clamp her shoulders and spin her back to him.

'Afraid, Georgina?'

His mocking tone brought her chin up, her eyes defiant. 'Why should I be afraid of you?'

The corners of his mouth quirked. 'Not me, my beautiful friend, but yourself. Of the feelings you're doing your best to stifle.'

'I don't know what you're talking about.' She kept her body rigid, her eyes cold, hiding the fire that raged deep inside.

'Oh, come, don't try and fool me.' His fingers began a gentle, seductive massage, his tone dropping an octave lower. 'Physically, you find me irresistible.'

Georgina's eyes widened. 'You conceited swine.' But she thanked her lucky stars that was all he thought. If he knew her emotions were involved he really would have something to laugh about. 'Let go of me, you brute, I hate you. I hate you, do you hear? Let me go.'

But her struggles were in vain; in fact they seemed to amuse him. His smile turned into a grin, and one hand slid behind her head, the other behind her back, imprisoning her against him.

'Did Robert kiss you tonight?' he asked, his eyes darkening as his mouth swooped down towards hers.

'I think that's my business,' she retorted coolly.

'Did he have the same effect on you that I'm having?'

'All you're doing is making me angry.' And sending her temperature soaring!

'Then I suggest you put all those passionate feelings into this kiss.' Before she could speak his mouth was on hers in a deliberate, sensual onslaught of her senses. Desire ran through her like quicksilver and although she tried her hardest to resist a few seconds was all she managed, a few seconds fighting the inevitable.

There was no tenderness in his kiss, instead a deep, urgent need, as though he were slaking a thirst he had denied for too long. And as all sane thoughts deserted her Georgina opened her mouth up to his, her arms snaking around him, moaning her pleasure at his deep and desperate exploration.

He drew away from her, a faint smile trembling on his lips. Georgina's legs were trembling too, her body fiery hot, her heart beating so hard that it hurt.

'I knew you'd come to your senses,' he mocked softly, and when he kissed her again the hardness had gone. This time his tongue and teeth tantalised and teased, seducing her emotions, making her burn with desire. He lifted her chin and ran his tongue down the smooth arch of her throat. Mindless whimpers escaped her and she buried her hands convulsively in his hair, holding him closer to her, not ever wanting him to stop.

Even when he inched her blouse out of her skirt and caressed the soft skin of her back she did not stop him, nor when he undid the clasp of her bra and moved his hand forward to take the soft fullness of her breast into his palm. She was beyond caring. His fingers sought and found her already hardened nipple and Georgina arched herself into him, feeling delirious with sheer pleasure.

Her breathing became erratic and difficult and her whole body was a mass of sensation. Everything but Leon faded into oblivion. There was nothing but him and his lovemaking and the primitive feelings he created.

His thighs were hard against hers, his arousal complete, and nothing else mattered.

'Georgina.' His voice was thick and desperate. 'Georgina, I want you.'

And she wanted him too, but somewhere in the sane part of her mind warning bells rang. 'No, Leon.'

'Yes, Georgina.'

'No!' She pushed away from him and her head rolled back as she looked up in panic. Her eyes still reflected the desire that gripped her but she was determined not to give way to it. A kiss was acceptable but she would go no further.

'It's what we both want.' His arm came back around her. 'You're as aroused as I am. You can't back out now.'

'I can, Leon, and I am.' Brave words, though her voice gave away her frustration.

'Dammit, Georgina, you can't do this to me. I won't let you.' His jaw was grim, the skin drawn tightly across his angular cheekbones. He looked as hurt and unhappy as she felt.

'You can't stop me.'

His fingers bit cruelly into her skin. 'You didn't stop me kissing you. You must have known what would happen the moment you saw me waiting.'

'I didn't,' she insisted, a pleading tone entering her voice.

'You thought you could call a halt just whenever you felt like it?'

She swallowed hard and nodded.

'Is that how you treat Robert? Do you hold out the tantalising carrot and then withdraw it at the last moment, when there's a danger of things getting too hot?' He did not let her answer. 'Well, my name's not Robert, and I allow no woman to make a fool of me.'

'I'm not trying to make a fool of you, Leon.'

'Then what is it you're doing?' His tone was controlled but she could sense his anger.

'I—I'm—it's self-preservation,' she burst out defensively. 'I can't go to bed with a man I despise.'

'A few seconds ago it didn't seem like that.'

'I got carried away. I'm sorry.'

'Sorry?' he scorned. 'Is saying you're sorry supposed to help?'

'Damn you, Leon,' she grated. 'What else can I say?'

His nostrils dilated as he glared into her eyes, his fingers still digging into her shoulders. 'You win—I have no intention of forcing myself on you. But, mark my words, you'll come begging me for it before much longer.'

'I don't think so,' said Georgina.

'I know so,' he told her firmly. 'I'll leave you now to sleep in your lonely little room, but one day you're going to be mine.'

Georgina collapsed on to the bed when he had gone, her thoughts a mangled mixture of relief and disappointment. She was glad she hadn't given in, yet conversely she felt frustrated. Emotions still raged inside her, a passion she had not known herself capable of feeling.

She felt humiliated too that she had revealed so much of herself to him, and knew that tomorrow would be painful. How was she ever going to face him again? She dragged off her clothes and pulled on her nightie, and then belatedly decided that she wanted to use the bathroom. Cautiously she opened her door and all was clear, but when she came out Leon was approaching and her heartbeat accelerated.

'Goodnight,' she said to him faintly as they passed each other, aware that his eyes had looked through the thin material to her naked body beneath.

'If you know what's best for you you won't parade around like that,' he growled.

Georgina already knew that it had been a mistake; she didn't need him telling her. She merely lifted her chin and walked as haughtily as was possible in bare feet and filmy nylon, shutting her door firmly and wishing there was a lock so that she could shut him out.

The rest of the week went by without her seeing very much of him. He went out every night and she could only assume it was Sheena who was taking up so much of his time. Was this his way of getting back at her? Georgina had never felt so depressed in her life. And then on Friday evening he suddenly said to her, 'Whatever your plans are for tomorrow, change them, because we're going out.'

'We?' A frown stabbed her brow at the same time as excitement rose inside her.

'That's right, you and I, just the two of us. A whole day spent together. Won't that be fun?'

'I have no wish to spend the day with you,' she said coldly, and it was the biggest lie she had ever told. She wanted to go, she wanted to with all her heart. But what was the point? It could lead only to heartache.

'You have no choice,' he told her firmly, and he meant it!

She took in a deep, unsteady breath. 'Where are we going?'

'On a picnic.'

It got worse.

'Make sure you're up early. I intend setting off at about eight.'

'Do you wish me to pack food?'

He waved his hand airily. 'That's all taken care of. Just bring something warm in case it gets chilly.'

Georgina slept fitfully that night, looking forward to the next day and yet not looking forward to it. She was mixed up where her feelings for Leon were concerned, and she certainly had no idea what was going on in his mind. Why had he asked her? Why not Sheena? Was it his intention to share himself between them? She did not want to share him, she wanted all of him or nothing. Why had she agreed to go? Why was she always weak where he was concerned?

She got up just before seven and took a shower and after much deliberation dressed in a pair of white cotton trousers and a pale green short-sleeved cotton top with a scooped neckline. She tucked a white sweatshirt into her canvas bag, together with hairbrush, suncream and tissues, and went down into the kitchen to make coffee and toast. Leon was already there.

'Ah, good, you're ready. I've made a pot of coffee if you'd like a cup.'

Georgina's raised eyebrows marked her surprise that he should be so polite. It was unlike him. 'Thank you.'

He poured it while she slotted bread into the toaster and for the first time in ages they sat together at the table. He was up to something, thought Georgina. He had virtually ignored her for several days and now this—and the prospect of probably twelve more hours in his company!

As soon as they had finished eating he suggested they leave, but when he drove down to the village and stopped the car she looked at him curiously.

'Come along,' he said, holding the door open for her to get out.

'What's going on?' she asked, suspicion in her tone. 'I thought we were going on a picnic?'

'So we are, but a picnic of a different kind.' He grinned widely and grabbed her hand, and she was compelled to walk with him as though she were a reluctant schoolgirl. The feelings that ran through her weren't like those of a child, however. The simple act of holding hands sent a whole host of sensations racing through her.

Suddenly she noticed the motor launch tied up at the pier and it was towards this that he dragged her.

'Ours for the day,' he informed her loftily, at the same time waving to Bob who was sitting in his customary position on the edge of the pier, puffing contentedly at his pipe.

Georgina acknowledged him too and saw the curiosity in his eyes. This is as much as surprise to me as it is to you, she wanted to tell him. More than a surprise, in fact, a shock. A picnic on a boat—as far away from anyone else as they could possibly get! What devious thoughts were going through Leon's mind now?

It wasn't an exceptionally big boat, though it was nicely shaped with long, sleek lines. It had a cabin that slept two, a tiny galley and a living and eating area. The wood was highly polished, the brass gleamed, and the paintwork was immaculate. 'It belongs to a friend of mine,' he explained, starting the engine and untying the ropes that anchored her to the pier.

'Do you know how to handle it?' Georgina herself knew nothing about boats of this sort.

'I'm not so stupid that I'd take her out if I didn't,' he answered drily, heading for the deeper waters in the middle of the loch and then along the length of the loch itself.

They circled the island she had admired from the rowing boat and there were other, smaller islands, each inviting inspection, but they were unable to get close enough. 'We could drop anchor and take the dinghy,' said Leon when she voiced her interest, 'but there are other more beautiful places to see.'

After another ten minutes' cruising Georgina thought they had reached the end of the loch, and was surprised to discover that where two outcrops of land almost met it opened out again into another much larger loch, easily a mile wide and the end was not in sight. 'I never knew,' she said, clapping her hands in childish delight.

Leon grinned and they followed the shoreline as close as they dared. 'This leads to the open sea, and the islands,' he informed her. 'Skye, Raasay, South Rona, Scalpay.'

'Wonderful,' she said. 'Can we visit one of them?' Already she was forgetting her trepidation over spending so much time alone with him. He was a different person. He was making her feel as though this day meant as much to him as it did to her. Sheena was forgotten, Robert was forgotten. It was just the two of them and nothing and no one else mattered. He was showing her sights and places she had never expected to see and she was enjoying every minute of it.

The land on either side of the loch was craggy and impressive and Georgina's eyes were all about her. She thought she spotted a golden eagle over the forested banks but couldn't be sure because she knew they weren't easily seen, and wasn't that an otter on the shore?

Silently she touched Leon's arm and pointed it out to him. He nodded and moved the throttle to the idle position and for a while they watched the sleek brown mammal playing in the shallows, and then just as suddenly he had gone, alerted by some smell or sound, possibly even themselves.

Georgina had not realised how closely she was standing to Leon as they watched the otter's antics and now, as he turned, his body brushed hers and a thousand tiny prickles shivered across her skin. She wanted to move away but some inner force compelled her to remain.

She looked at his hands on the wheel, strong hands with a fine coating of brown hairs, square-tipped fingers with well-manicured nails. There was nothing weak about them, they were a part of his powerful, masterful whole—and they had touched her so intimately a few nights ago!

The thought brought a quick surge of warmth, an instant stampede of her pulses. She looked away from him, up at the clouds hurried by the wind across an azure sky, but when her eyes came back to him he was watching her and there was something in his expression that tightened her throat and brought an ache to her loins.

There had been raw need, a physical desire for her, and although it had been blanked immediately she could not ignore what she had seen. 'Shall I make us some coffee?' she asked, feeling a need to put space between them, startled to hear how husky and breathless her voice sounded.

'Perhaps that might be a good idea,' he said, his tone also deeper and gruffer than she had ever heard.

She felt as though she had to wrench herself away from him. In those few minutes they had developed a to-getherness not experienced before. It had felt good and right being so close to him, yet she knew the insanity of letting such a situation develop. He would take her and use her but he would never love her—not as she loved him!

In the galley, out of his sight, she closed her eyes, needing a few moments to regain her equilibrium. It was going to be a long, difficult day. She dared not give herself away—it would lead only to her destruction.

She put the kettle on to boil and, reaching in the refrigerator for milk, she saw a bottle of champagne—Dom Perignon, no less. It was going to be some picnic, she thought.

Once the coffee was made she took it out to him but this time she moved to the other side of the cockpit, making a pretence of watching their bow-wave. How else was she to keep her eyes off him?

But after a few minutes of silence she was drawn back to him, turning to sit on the slatted seat, watching him as he steered the boat on its course. He was looking straight ahead, seeming not to notice her change of position. Only when he spoke did she find out that he had seen her every move.

'Do you feel safer over there, Georgina?' A mocking smile accompanied his words.

'I don't know what you mean.'

'Oh, I think you do.' His hands splayed lightly on the wheel, as though he were caressing her breasts, and his large teeth gleamed white in his suntanned face. His was the predatory grin of a hunter—and she was his prey! 'I think you find my nearness too disturbing for comfort.'

'Is that surprising?' she countered.

'Not at all. You're simply running true to course.'

She frowned. 'What are you talking about?'

'We both know that we shall end up as lovers.'

Georgina felt a swift plummet of disappointment. She had been right—all he was interested in was an affair, nothing more.

'You're simply playing the age-old game and keeping me waiting.'

'No, I am not,' she returned heatedly.

'No?'

The cool insolence of his gaze triggered fresh sensations and Georgina wondered how much of this she could handle. The day had only just begun and already he had caused her body to panic. She couldn't possibly last out for another eight or so hours.

She took a sip of her coffee and hung on to her mug, cradling it in her hands, wishing it were Leon's neck. Sometimes she thought she hated him as much as she loved him.

He said no more but the smile never left his face and he whistled softly as he steered them on their course. He was wearing grey canvas shoes and close-fitting cords, which emphasised his slim hips and hard, flat stomach. His white cotton shirt was halfway open, revealing his deeply tanned chest. There wasn't an ounce of superfluous flesh on him. He was all hard, trim, muscle— and at this moment he was getting a kick out of her discomfort.

Finishing her coffee, she took their two mugs and washed them up. Maybe she could stay down here? she thought, looking around her at the cabin with its brown velour seats and toning chintz curtains. But that thought died the instant it was born.

'Georgina, what are you doing? Come up here, I want your company.'

Reluctantly she obeyed his command.

'What was keeping you?'

She shrugged. 'I was looking around.'

He nodded as if satisfied. 'A nice boat, don't you think?'

'Who does it belong to?'

'Iain Stewart, but it's up for sale because he doesn't have time to use it since taking over the inn. I'm considering buying it for use of the hotel guests. What do you think?'

Georgina looked at him with raised brows. 'Would my opinion count?'

'But of course.'

She didn't believe him but thought it a good idea anyway and told him so. 'You could even let it out to people who want a cruising holiday.'

He inclined his head. 'A brilliant suggestion. Would you like to have a go at the wheel?'

Instinctively Georgina shook her head. 'I don't think so. I've never handled a boat this size.'

'It's quite easy, I'll show you. Come on.'

She was left with no choice. 'This is the throttle.' He put her hand on it, covering it with his own, leaving it there long enough to send prickles of awareness through her. 'The rest is simply a matter of steering as you would a car. Take it nice and easy and you'll have no problem.'

His arm was across the back of her shoulders, his legs touching hers. She was thankful they weren't wearing shorts; she would not have been able to suffer naked flesh against naked flesh. As it was she could feel the heat of his body and it sent her own temperature soaring.

Even when she thought she was doing nicely he still stood there, sending her pulses crazy and her adrenalin pumping. 'I think I've got the hang of it now,' she said, hoping he might move, but she might as well not have spoken.

'You can go in a bit closer here,' he said.

She turned the wheel and immediately his hand came over hers. 'More gently, Georgina. You're not steering a tank.'

But he was bulldozing through her feelings as though sublimely unaware of the chaos he was creating. Or was it deliberate? She guessed it was. This assault on her senses was carefully worked out. He knew she had no escape from him now and even if she did make a mistake at the wheel they would come to no harm out here on this vast expanse of water.

She clenched her teeth and concentrated on what she was doing. 'Relax.' The word was muttered softly in her ear, his body half bent over her. 'You're as tense as a string on a violin.'

And she would be for as long as he stood there. Five minutes went by, ten, a quarter of an hour. He had straightened but not moved, he was looking around him, the wind ruffling his hair, a silent whistle pursing his lips. His bruise had almost gone and the scab had come off his cut, leaving a light pink scar.

'You can take over again,' she said when she could stand it no longer.

'Had enough already?' The smile that accompanied his words told her that he knew her reason.

'I think we're coming to the open sea. I don't feel confident enough to tackle that.' It was a lie and the truth all at the same time.

'The Inner Sound,' he corrected. 'We'll drop anchor near South Rona and hopefully spot some seals.'

Once he had seated himself at the wheel Georgina moved away and breathed more easily. Leon looked across at her and grinned and he seemed to know exactly how she felt.

When Georgina glanced at her watch she was amazed. It was almost twelve and they seemed to have been going only a short time.

'Hungry?' He asked.

She shook her head.

'We'll eat when we drop anchor. Another hour perhaps, does that suit you?'

'Whatever you wish,' she shrugged, turning away to lean over the rail and watch the churning waters. This was certainly going to be a day to remember.

They ate their food outside on the deck. The picnic hamper that had already been placed on the boat before they boarded was bulging with food. Dainty smoked salmon sandwiches, Scotch eggs, salad, petticoat tails. The champagne was uncorked and sat in a silver ice-bucket at their side. They had linen napkins. It was all very elegant and civilised.

Then they spotted the seals and spent an hour or two watching them and neither noticed the thunder-clouds building up until a few drops of rain fell. 'It looks as if we're in for a storm,' announced Leon. 'We'll take shelter in the lee of the island.'

Storms terrified Georgina. Her brothers had jeered at her and called her a sissy and she had tried her hardest to overcome her fear, but it was something she had never been able to control. And now, as she felt the familiar tension taking hold of her, she left Leon, hurriedly going down into the relative security of the cabin.

He was heading for a bay that would save them the worst of the storm but even before he reached it the rain hurled down in sheets and the wind churned the sea, buffeting and tossing the little craft as though she were made of matchwood. Georgina clung to the edge of the seat and prayed they would make it to safety.

Leon dropped anchor as the first lightning flash jagged the sky. Georgina put her hands over her ears and buried her face in the cushion, waiting for the crash of thunder to follow. Leon's hand touched her shoulder at exactly the same time and she cried out her fear.

Instinctively she turned and clung to him, heedless of his soaking shirt, holding him to her with all her strength.

'Georgina,' he said with a new softness to his tone. 'Georgina, it's all right.'

She turned to look at him. 'I'm sorry, I can't help it. I'm terrified of storms.' She hated to admit it to him. 'It's the only thing I'm really frightened of.'

'Let me get out of these wet clothes,' he said, prising her gently away. Without a hint of self-consciousness he peeled off his shirt and trousers, his shoes and socks. Even his underpants were wet and they came off too. He plucked a large towel from the bathroom and rubbed himself roughly dry before fastening it sarong-wise around his waist.

Georgina was too much in the grip of terror to feel uncomfortable and when the next lightning flash came she sprang into Leon's arms. 'Hold me, hold me,' she cried, her voice quivering with fear. 'Please don't let me go.'

CHAPTER NINE

THE roll of thunder followed quickly. The storm was getting nearer. Georgina felt panic well up and she buried her head into Leon's chest. It was hard and warm and hair-roughened and it represented safety. She would be all right while he held her.

'It's my fault,' he said. 'I should have listened to the radio for possible gale warnings. I shouldn't have brought the boat out.' But it had blown up out of nowhere and would probably go just as quickly.

He stroked her hair, murmuring words of comfort and encouragement. He did not laugh at her fears or call her a baby like her brothers. He seemed to understand and cradled her to him, and when the next spear of lightning lit the tiny cabin and the thunder reverberated directly overhead he covered her eyes with his hands and held her strongly and protectively against him.

Crash followed upon crash, seeming never-ending. Georgina trembled and quailed and clung desperately to Leon and his strength never failed. Even when the storm began to move away, when the lightning and thunder were less intense and less often, he still held her within the safety of his arms.

Now she began to grow aware of him, to feel the steady thud of his heart and the warmth of him and his sexuality which always shrouded him like a mantle, and when she dared to open her eyes he was looking at her.

His mouth was soft, his eyes compassionate. 'Feeling better?' he asked gruffly.

She twisted her lips wryly and nodded. 'I'm sorry. I seem to have made a complete fool of myself.' The cabin was filled with an eerie yellow light as the storm clouds receded and the sun fought bravely to show its face.

'Nonsense. It's a relief to find something that fazes you. I don't like women who are always in control of themselves.'

Another distant thunder-roll sent a fresh shudder through her limbs and she hid her face once again in his chest. It was more than two hours that they sat together, he protecting, she cowering, and finally, when it was all over, she was reluctant to move away from him, though she knew that she must.

The sky had cleared, the sun shone, but Leon seemed in no hurry to let her go. They sat for ages, silently gathering their thoughts, enjoying the feel of each other's bodies, aware of the aura of sensuality that drew them together.

'I think,' said Leon at length, his tone no louder than the chuckle of water against their bow, 'that it's too late to go home now. I think we should stay here.'

Immediately Georgina stiffened. It was one thing feeling this rapport, this togetherness, wishing it would go on for ever, but another to have Leon suggesting they spend the night together. 'I don't think that's necessary, Leon. Stramore's not that far away. We can make it before dark.'

'The storm might flare up again,' he said at once. In the far distance they could still hear the faintly ominous roll of thunder. 'At least we're sheltered. I think it's by far the most sensible thing to do.'

Georgina drew in a deep breath and reluctantly agreed. 'I suppose you're right.'

'I know I am,' he grinned.

'I'll make us some coffee,' she said in a strangled voice, peeling herself away from him and trailing out into the galley where she sloshed water into the kettle and set it on the gas stove, tapping her fingers nervously on top of the cupboard as she waited for it to boil. This was going to be more difficult than she had expected. A whole night here together! Anything could happen. And she was in no frame of mind to stop him.

She thrust his mug at him when the coffee was made. He still wore the towel, his shirt and trousers drying on hangers, and there was amusement on his face when he said, 'Something tells me you're not too happy with the arrangement?'

'I'm not,' she muttered.

'Why, because there's no escape? Or——' a frown furrowed his brow '—are you wishing I were Robert? Would that suit you better?' A sudden harshness entered his voice.

She turned her head away. 'It's not that, it's—it doesn't seem right.'

'Really? What's the difference between us being here or in the hotel together?'

'There's only one cabin. I can't sleep in there with you. I'd rather sleep under the stars.'

'That's your prerogative.'

Her eyes widened. 'You mean you'd let me?'

'Let's say I wouldn't try to dissuade you if you were that foolish. Sit down and drink your coffee.'

'No, thanks.' She needed space to breathe, to clear her head from the insane thoughts that spun inside it. He was so very, very dear to her, and yet this was all a game to him.

She took her mug outside and stood and looked out at the island. South Rona was tiny and Leon had told her that it was inhabited only by the lighthouse keepers.

Further on was Raasay, fifteen miles long with a very uneven coastline. She contemplated taking the dinghy but wasn't sure whether she would be able to get in close enough to the shore without damaging the boat. She was stuck here whether she liked it or not.

'What are you thinking?'

Georgina spun around, surprised to find him behind her, and her natural good humour came flooding to the surface. She grinned. 'Have you got a pack of cards? I thought we could while away the hours until bedtime playing poker.'

He frowned. 'Are you serious?'

She nodded.

'I don't believe this, a man and a girl alone out at sea on a boat and they *play cards*? Unless——' a gleam came into his eyes '—it's strip poker you're thinking of?'

'Trust you to think of something like that,' flashed Georgina. 'Have you forgotten that you're undressed already? I'll go and see if I can find a pack.'

Leon followed her, leaning laconically against the door-frame, watching with amused eyes as she opened cupboards and drawers.

'There are none,' she said, her tone disappointed.

'Then we'll have to make up our own games.'

Her eyes met his and she wilted beneath the intentness of his gaze.

'I suggest,' he said, 'that we sit out there on the deck and you can tell me all about yourself, about your childhood, about your innermost thoughts and secrets. I want to know everything about you.'

Georgina wasn't so sure about that, but at least outside she wouldn't feel his suffocating presence quite so much. Those long minutes spent locked in his arms had told her how easily she could be influenced by him, how easily her feelings came flooding to the surface.

Leon mopped the deck dry before laying out a towel for her to sit on. It was really quite warm considering the storm. She leaned back on her elbows and closed her eyes, wondering how she had ever let herself get into this situation.

She could sense him watching and an impossible warmth stole through her veins. It made no difference being out here in the open air. Every nerve and fibre responded and she ached for him to hold her again. The love she had for Leon was growing stronger by the day, by the minute. Soon she would be unable to deny it.

'Do you ever wish you'd had any sisters, Georgina?'

She opened her eyes and looked at him and he was sitting so close she could see every pore in his face and the clear greyness of his eyes and his brows which grew thick and bushy. 'Occasionally, not often.'

'I wonder, if you had one, whether she'd have this same glorious chestnut hair?' As he spoke he twisted a length of her hair through his fingers, bending low to bury his nose in its thickness. 'It smells beautiful. Which side of your family does it come from?'

Georgina did not know how she was expected to answer when his closeness threatened her sanity. It had been different when she was consumed by fear; now she was filled with the musky smell of him, with his potent masculinity, and it was difficult to think coherently. 'My mother's,' she managed, a husky tremor in her voice. 'Though my mother was blonde—it was my grandmother who had hair like mine.'

'I love it.' He wound the lock round his fingers and used it to pull himself even closer to her.

'I'm glad there's something about me that you like,' she managed to quip.

'Oh, there are lots of things, believe me,' he answered, his voice throbbing low in his throat now. 'You're one hell of an attractive lady, Georgina. You must know that. I can understand why my nephew fell for you. Tell me, did he stir your blood as I do?'

She closed her eyes and thought about her answer carefully. 'I can't tell you that, Leon. There's no comparison. You're two totally different people.' The honest reply would have been no. Craig had left her cold compared to the chaotic emotions Leon aroused.

'Did your pulses quiver when he touched you? Did your heart go bump when he looked at you—as it's doing now?' As if to prove a point he placed his hand over her heart. 'Feel it, it's like a traction engine.' He took her hand and put it beneath his and she felt her own powerful response to him.

That, combined with his hand over hers, created utter confusion inside her. 'It's nothing,' she protested. 'It's a perfectly natural reaction to a man as strongly sexual as you.'

'Even if that man has turned your life upside down? Come, Georgina, you'll have to do better than that.'

She twisted from him, willing him to go away, to at least stop talking in this vein.

'Coward.' The word danced softly on the air and she pretended not to hear.

'Do you know what I think?' His face was close to her ear now. 'I think that every one of your veins is singing; I think that it's more than physical attraction that you feel for me. God knows why after the way I've treated you. But that's what I think. Am I right?'

'You couldn't be further from the truth,' she answered, keeping her tone deliberately sharp, though it was difficult when she wanted to turn and press herself into him. She almost wished for the storm to return so that she would have a valid excuse. She wanted to be a part of him, she wanted to belong, and it was all so hard because he felt nothing for her. He was playing with her, teasing her. He found her attractive, she did not doubt that, but it meant nothing. Absolutely nothing.

'I think we should carry out a little experiment.'

Georgina's widened. 'Such as what?'

In answer he lowered his head, his mouth ready for hers. She knew what could and would happen if she allowed the kiss. Swiftly she turned her head, but he was expecting it and his fingers gripped her chin, his lips closing over hers with a similar hunger to the one that had raged inside her all day.

'Leon . . .' She managed to free herself for a moment.

'Relax, my sweet girl, let your heart rule your head for a change.' He breathed the words into her mouth.

'But Leon . . .'

'You want me, I know you do. You've been wanting me all day even though you've done your very best not to show it.'

As his mouth closed over hers again she shut her eyes. Why bother to protest when he took no notice? Why bother when she wanted his kiss anyway?

It felt as though her whole body was being set on fire. He triggered off sensations that made her senses spin and time lose all meaning. Her tension slid away like a moon behind a cloud, her mouth opened to his like the unfurling petals of a rose.

Her arms went around him and he laid her gently down. Her body pressed close to his, tiny whispering sounds of pleasure and satisfaction escaping the back of her throat. She did not stop to wonder what she was doing; it was a time for senses and feelings, a time to feel free of the self-erected chains of defence that had bound her for so long.

'That's better.' His low, mesmeric tone sent a fresh thrill riding along her spine. 'Never fight the inevitable, Georgina.'

She swallowed his breathing and accepted his now deepening kiss. He was right, it was inevitable. Right from the very beginning, from the moment they had met at the cocktail party, she had been aware of his magnetism, had felt his strength and power. Except that she had thought it was mutual, until time had told her differently. Even if the Craig incident hadn't occurred it would have made no difference. She would have lasted no longer than any of the others.

But she could fight him no longer. She would take whatever crumbs of love he cared to throw to her. No, not love, never love. Not on his part. Lust. That was the word. Pure, unadulterated sex.

But how beautiful it was, how perfectly their bodies moulded together, how much she ached for him, how swiftly her blood flowed. Their tongues touched and explored, her throat arched as she lifted herself to him and his mouth burnt a trail down its pulsating length. His hand moved to the soft cotton of her T-shirt, pushing it up, searching for and finding the proud mounds of her breasts, exposing them to the air so that she felt marvellously free. She even lifted her body so that he could take her top off altogether, and then lay back down in sweet surrender.

First one and then the other aching nipple was taken into his mouth. He sucked and bit and teased and tormented until she felt that she was going out of her mind. Her eyes were still tight closed, her body squirming, her groin aching, her throat contracted so that her breathing was as heavy as if she had run a four-minute mile.

When he raised his head to look at her his eyes were glazed, his mouth soft and wet, his lips dark. 'You're irresistible, Georgina. Wonderfully, beautifully, totally feminine. Kiss me, tell me you want me. Oh, God, tell me you want me.'

Georgina thrilled at the need in his voice, at the vibrant, throbbing hunger. It matched her own, surpassed it even, and she wanted, above all else, to fulfil that need for him. She felt almost faint with sensation, her head light and floating away, her body not belonging to herself any more, but to Leon, only to Leon.

'Georgina?'

She pulled his head back down to her breasts so that he could not speak, so that he could not spoil this magical moment with words, and she buried her fingers into the thickness of his hair, feeling the shape of him, wanting to hold him against her for ever.

His teeth bit, he sucked her deeply into his mouth, and it felt as though he wanted to swallow her breasts, that he wanted to eat her little bit by little bit. It was a calculated seduction of her senses and her hips writhed and her whole body arched upwards. *'Leon!'* His name was torn out of her mouth, her fingers knotted in his hair, transferring her desperation to him.

His hand took the place of his mouth at her breast and once again he captured her eager, hungry lips, and there was no tenderness in the kiss now, nothing but a mutual heat and passion, the thirst of two people lost in the wilderness of their own desire.

Yet even so Georgina did not entirely lose control of her senses. When his hand moved with calculated slowness from her breasts to her midriff, from her midriff to her stomach, and then touched the fastening on her trousers, she murmured a faint protest, drowned by the roar of desire in her ears.

Leon hesitated and then slipped the button undone, sliding down the zipper with expert fingers. Georgina fought an inner battle with herself and won. 'No, Leon.'

Still her tone was quiet, but it was firm and he stopped. 'You're right, we'd be far more comfortable in bed.' With the speed of the lightning that had split the skies earlier he lifted her up into his arms and Georgina's protests were ignored.

The bunk was firm, but softer than the hard deck which had bruised her spine and Georgina lay where Leon had put her, looking up into the face which she had grown to love. She no longer resisted. Leon had once said that he would not force her, that any initiative would have to come from her, and with the heat of her passion unslaked she looked at him now with glowing eyes.

She was not aware in that moment that she was revealing every intimate thought and desire; she was aware only of her own arousal. His hard body had brushed against her naked breasts as he carried her inside, he had looked down at her with the exquisite pain of need in his eyes, and her protests had faded like the dying embers of a fire.

This time she allowed him to slide her trousers off, followed by the scraps of lace that were her briefs, until she lay completely naked, quivering under the scrutiny of his eyes. Brief though his appraisal was, he did not miss one inch of her anatomy and she felt as though she were being examined under a microscope. 'Beautiful, quite beautiful,' he said softly, and the towel fell from his loins.

Georgina feasted her eyes on him, seeing him now, her eyes no longer glazed with fear. She saw his powerful physique, the sheen of tanned skin stretched tautly over muscle and bone. He was in perfect physical shape and she wanted him with a desperation that both shocked and frightened her.

His lovemaking was all and more than she had ever dreamt. He was a tender and considerate lover, arousing her to heights unimagined, soaring with her, bringing their lovemaking to a pinnacle, to a final, shattering, explosive ecstasy.

Afterwards they slept wrapped in each other's arms, and when Georgina opened her eyes the last streaks of daylight were leaving the sky. Almost midnight, she thought. In a few hours there would be the dawn of another day and her life would take on a whole new meaning.

She had given herself to Leon freely and willingly. It had been her own conscious choice and it meant he now held her in the palm of his hand—to either destroy or accept her love. She suspected it would be the former and she felt sad that the happiness she had experienced beneath Leon's hands could not last.

'You look despondent, little one.'

Georgina had not realised he was awake and she turned her head to look at him. His smooth, hard body was close to hers in the narrow bunk, inciting fresh flames of passion, and he had the sleepy, lazy look of a sated lion. But she did not underestimate him; that would be fatal.

'Are you thinking that in a few short hours all this will be over? That we will be back at the hotel with our separate bedrooms?'

'No.' She decided to answer him honestly. 'I was wondering whether you're satisfied now that you've—taken me? Whether the whole object of the exercise was my humiliation and from now on our relationship will revert to what it's been for the last few weeks?'

A harsh frown was quickly banished. 'Is that what you want?' He traced a line from her forehead, down her nose and over her lips and Georgina had to restrain herself hard from grabbing his hand and kissing it. She must never again appear so eager.

'I don't suppose what I want enters into it.'

'Tell me.'

How could she, when it was Leon's love she craved? Again she turned her head away. 'It doesn't matter.'

'You think I'm a cold, uncaring swine who doesn't give a damn about you?'

The sudden brusque tones of his voice made her shrink away but he turned her head back, his fingers hard now, using the force she always connected with him. 'Georgina, strange as this may seem, I do have a heart. I never make love just for the sheer hell of it.'

'You mean you actually feel something for me?' Joy rose swiftly inside her; she had underestimated him, he did care. He loved her!

'In my own way, yes.'

Disappointment now took the place of joy. It wasn't love he felt, they both knew that. It wasn't a feeling that would last. She was here and available—and willing! And that was all there was to it. He was after an affair. Whether it lasted three months or three years made no difference. He wouldn't offer her marriage at the end of it. She had been a fool to ever let him see how he affected her. She should have kept a resolute distance, doing her work to the best of her ability, but otherwise keeping out of his way. Throwing herself at him during the thunderstorm had been the worst thing she could have possibly done.

She looked at him coldly. 'Ironically the feeling's not mutual. I feel nothing at all for you, Leon.'

His body grew tense and he withdrew from her. 'You mean you'd give yourself to any man who attracted you physically? Have you given yourself to Robert?' This last sentence was snapped out viciously. 'Have you, Georgina?'

'No, no!' she cried at once. 'I'm not like that, I wouldn't do that.'

'Then why...?'

'Don't ask me,' she said quickly. 'I made a mistake, one I shall regret for the rest of my life.'

She saw the muscle jerking in his jaw, the hard anger that tautened his skin and wondered why he was reacting so strongly.

The bed felt empty when he left her, springing up as if the thought of her by his side was now distasteful. He went through to the tiny bathroom. She heard the shower and all the time she lay there and wondered what was going to happen to them. When he came back he climbed into the bunk opposite, pulled the sheet over him, and a few minutes later his deepened breathing told her that he was asleep.

How could he sleep when something as momentous as this had happened? She sat up, leaning back against the bulkhead, her hands clasped around her knees. All the beautiful, warm feelings had gone, replaced with sadness, regret that with a few words she had put an end to what could have been a beautiful relationship. She consoled herself with the thought that the cost of going on with it would have been much too high. She wanted Leon to be a part of her life for ever.

Helen had warned her against him, had told her that he dated many girls, and she had seen proof of it herself with Sheena. So why had she let him make love to her? What a fool she had been. As far as Leon was concerned it had been a bodily function, nothing more. A need fulfilled.

Resting her head back, she closed her eyes, her legs straightened, but she did not relax. She sat there with her thoughts until the shadow of night was pushed back and the light of a new day dawned. It was still early, far too early to get up, and as the little cabin grew lighter she looked at the sleeping man in the other bunk.

He was so close she had only to lean over to touch him. He lay on his back, his black hair tousled, the harsh lines of his face softened. He looked younger, not so formidable. He was covered to his waist only by the sheet and his tightly muscled chest moved up and down as he breathed. She had to resist the urge to reach out and run her hand over his hair-roughened skin. This was probably the one and only time she would see him like this and she tried to imprint every tiny detail into her memory.

For two hours she watched him. He turned once and muttered something unintelligible and she could tell by the rapid movements behind his eyelids that he was dreaming, and then when it was almost six o'clock he opened his eyes and looked at her.

She saw the hardness steal over him, the mask that formed and hid the man who had made love to her, the man she had seen sleeping as contentedly as a new-born baby. 'Despite everything you still find me fascinating?' His nostrils flared as he flung the words caustically at her.

'Not exactly fascinating,' she was stung to retort, self-consciously pulling the sheet up over her breasts. 'I was simply wondering what makes a man like you tick. You're like a chameleon the way your moods change.'

'My moods are controlled by the people I meet. I have ambition, I admit that, and maybe I'm guilty of being ruthless—but only in a business sense. Basically I'm happy, kind, and considerate.'

'Really?' She took no pains to hide her sarcasm.

'And I don't use women for my own ends. You were as willing as me, and don't try to deny it.'

'Yes, I was willing,' she admitted. 'I fell prey to your charm. It was a fatal mistake.' She wondered what they looked like. Two naked people in two separate beds, each hungering for the other but separated by a great divide. It was an incongruous situation considering that a few short hours earlier they had made love. 'I should have believed Helen when she said you were a philanderer.'

A frown stabbed his brow. 'She said that?'

Georgina nodded.

'Sour grapes, I imagine, because I wouldn't have anything to do with her. I prefer to choose my own girlfriends, not have them choose me.'

'You also told me yourself that you had no intention of getting serious with anyone else.'

His jaw tensed. 'Yes, I said that, and I meant it.'

'So why did you make love to me?'

'Why did you let me?'

She knew that both answers were the same. They had both been driven by something beyond their power. A raw need deep inside them. Neither could blame the other.

'This is an impossible situation,' she said bluntly.

'I agree.'

'We should never have stayed out here overnight.'

'I don't think the place makes any difference. It could have happened anywhere, at any time. I have no regrets, Georgina.'

'Well, I have,' she snapped. 'I don't like to think of myself as another one of your statistics.'

His mouth went taut, his eyes glacial. 'Damn your friend Helen.'

'Don't blame her; I've seen for myself what you're like. You're having fun with Sheena as well as me. Have you made love to her yet? I know she'd be willing. She thinks the sun shines out of your eyes.'

He snorted angrily. 'This is a most ridiculous conversation.' He pushed himself up out of bed. Georgina turned away. Maybe he wasn't embarrassed by his nudity, but she was. Not last night, not when feelings and sensations had meant more than anything else, but now, when the fires of his desire had burnt out, she felt offended by his overt masculinity.

The next time Georgina saw him his jaw was freshly shaven and he smelled of his familiar musk. He wore the same grey pants but a clean white shirt and a fresh spurt of anger ripped through her. 'You planned all this, didn't you? If it hadn't been the storm you would have found some other excuse for staying out the night.'

'The Fates were kind,' he agreed pleasantly.

Georgina was also washed and dressed, but in the same clothes, even the same underclothes, and without any make-up. She had found a new toothbrush in the bathroom and now knew exactly why it had been there. It all became clear. Making love to her had been a part of his plan all along.

'I hate you, Leon Alexander,' she spat. 'I hate you with every fibre of my being. Get this boat going—I want to go home.'

A muscle jerked in his jaw, giving away his inner tension, even though he seemed amused. 'Do you know what, Georgina? You're mine now. Mine in every sense of the word, and I have no intention of letting you go, ever.'

CHAPTER TEN

GEORGINA'S green eyes flashed fire. 'Strong words, Mr Alexander, but there's no way you can hold me against my will. I've stayed too long already.'

Leon's mouth curled into a confident smile. 'Who said anything about forcing you? You're forgetting your emotions. They will hold you by me side even though you profess to hate me.'

'Rubbish!' she thrust heatedly, at the same time recognising the truth behind his words. 'I'd be a poor example of my sex if I let my emotions rule my life.'

'You won't be the first and you won't be the last.'

She shook her head angrily and the sun streaming through the window shot her hair with a million different hues of red and gold. It was her most flamboyant feature and in that moment, with the sun behind her, her hair looked almost as if it were on fire.

Leon's eyes were narrowed and watchful and he moved towards her as though pulled by a magnet stronger than life itself. His eyes were fixed on her hair, mesmerised by its luminescence, his hands reaching out to touch and marvel and admire and Georgina found that she could not move a muscle.

Even beset by an anger so deep that it enflamed every bone in her body she still could not resist him, could not deny him the right to touch her. She remained frozen to the spot, suffering his almost reverent caress. 'I've never met a girl with such beautiful hair,' he murmured. 'It is quite magnificent.' He palmed its weight each side of her head, lifting it so that the sunlight filtered through, illuminating each hair like the gossamer strands of a spider's web.

The longer he stood there the quicker her anger melted, pure sexual desire taking its place. In the end she could stand it no longer and she whirled away. 'What are we going to have for breakfast?' Not that she was hungry; her throat was so tight she felt sure she couldn't swallow the tiniest morsel.

'Coffee and toast, and I'll do it. You sit there and look beautiful.'

'No!' Georgina shook her head emphatically. 'I'll make it, you start the engine. We'll eat while we're moving.'

But he would have none of it. 'What's the rush? It's Sunday and there isn't a cloud in the sky. Let's enjoy it while we can. We're having an extraordinary summer, don't you think?'

Small talk designed to take her mind off the real issue. Georgina clamped her lips and lifting the kettle off the stove began to fill it. 'I don't suppose I have any choice.' She never did. 'But I'll still make breakfast.'

She found a loaf of bread that had nothing to do with yesterday's picnic, and she toasted some of it and spread it with butter and marmalade. She made a jug of coffee, and piling everything on to a tray, took it outside. Leon was on the deck and he leaned down and lifted it from her. The sun was warm already and it was indeed an idyllic day but she did not want to spend it with him. It had been a pleasant interlude but she wanted to put an end to it as quickly as possible.

Across in the distance the sun glinted on the light-house, and on the shore closer at hand she thought she saw a lone seal but could not be sure. Gulls wheeled and squealed and searched for food, and Leon spent his time looking at her.

It was unnerving, being constantly under surveillance, and she took refuge in pouring their coffee.

'Toast?' he asked, holding out the plate.

'No, thanks, I'm not hungry.'

He frowned. 'You must eat.'

So she took a slice but only nibbled it.

'Are you truly unhappy, Georgina?'

She eyed him warily. 'What sort of a question is that? Do you mean at this moment, or generally?'

'Are you unhappy working for me? Being with me, living with me?' His eyes were intent on her face as he spoke.

Georgina lowered her head, avoiding his eyes, knowing he would see too much. 'I'm happy in my work,' she admitted. 'I always am. But I'm not happy about our living arrangements.' She was too afraid of giving herself away, especially now. She felt more vulnerable than ever.

'You can go back to the cottage if you like.' A muscle flinched in his jaw as he spoke, as though it was difficult for him to make the offer.

Georgina knew it would be the safest and wisest thing to do, yet even so she found herself saying, 'I don't really want to do that. I like it where I am. I just—I just want you to—to leave me alone.' She did not look at him as she spoke, she looked down at the slice of toasted bread, at the marmalade, succulent and golden, and saw to her surprise that her hand was trembling. A tell-tale sign— he would know that she was lying. He always knew what she was feeling. It seemed at times that he could see into her very soul.

'You're asking the impossible.' His response came out as a soft growl. 'Have you any idea, Georgina, how irresistible you are?'

'I won't be your plaything.'

'I don't want you to be that. I want you to be yourself.'

Meaning he wanted her to let herself go, to let all the desires and cravings that he incited spill out. She swallowed hard. 'I'll stay as long as I'm able, but if things become too—uncomfortable, then I shall move back to the cottage for however long completion of Stramore House takes.'

He was a long time considering her proposal, so long in fact that Georgina thought he was going to have second thoughts and tell her to get out of his life altogether. It was surprising how much the thought hurt.

He finished his coffee and sat looking at the dregs in the bottom of the cup. Perhaps they should have had tea, thought Georgina. They might have read their future in the leaves. As far as she was concerned there was no future. Love him she might, but he had treated her abominably and in the end they would part. It was inevitable.

'It looks as though I have no choice but to accept your terms,' he said.

Georgina's lips flickered into a weak smile. 'If we both try hard I'm sure we won't regret it.' She felt almost on the verge of tears. If only it were love instead of lust that he felt for her.

After that he seemed in a hurry to move, finishing his breakfast and carrying the tray back down to the galley, starting the engine and pulling up anchor while Georgina washed up.

She almost wished she had not said anything. Despite being worried by the way their relationship was developing, she preferred Leon's warmth to his hostility. The rest of the day would be hell. Perhaps he would go straight home?

But when she joined him in the cockpit and looked around they were heading in the opposite direction, Rona and Raasay on one side of them, the dragon-ridged outline of Skye on the other. She thought he might drop anchor at Portree so that they could explore Skye, but he kept straight on, finally rounding the southernmost tip of Raasay and making his way back up the Inner Sound.

It seemed a pointless trip to Georgina when neither of them spoke, and when she could stand his silent company no longer she fetched a towel and lay down on the deck in the sunshine. The sky was flecked now with high white clouds looking like balls of spun sugar, with no sign at all of the storm that had raged yesterday, the storm that had sent her into his arms and started it all off.

A slow warmth traced its way through her as she thought about Leon's lovemaking. It wasn't going to be possible to live with him and keep her feelings hidden, she knew that. They were far too intense. She closed her eyes and, with the heat of the sun and the lack of sleep last night, felt herself drifting off to sleep.

She was awakened by Leon's hand on her arm and her eyes shot wide. 'What's wrong?'

'Nothing, but I've made us some lunch and I think you've been in the sun long enough.' His tone was gentle but his eyes were expressionless.

He held out a hand and she hung on and pulled herself up, but he let her go immediately and as she followed him down into the cabin a shiver ran through her. If this was what it was going to be like, cold indifference, then most definitely she could not live with him.

As soon as they had finished eating he set off again. They reached Stramore at a little before five and were back in the hotel shortly afterwards. Georgina went straight up to her room and threw herself down on the bed. What she ought to do was walk out on him right now and go home, except that her conscience would not let her go until the job was finished.

Work became her panacea. In the days and weeks that followed Leon did not give her a minute's peace. Check this, change that, an amendment here, an addition there. She fell into bed so tired at night that sleep claimed her immediately. Occasionally she caught him looking at her, and then her heart would race and her pulses leap and she would wait for him to say something, but he never did. His face always tightened into its mask of indifference and he turned his attention to the next job.

Robert was a regular visitor to her studio and he never failed to ask her out. But always she refused. There was no point in hurting him further. She would never, ever feel for him what she did for Leon.

'Forget him, Gina,' he said one day. 'You can't make him love you.'

'You can't make me love you either,' she whispered sadly.

He shrugged. 'That's true, but while there's no one else in your life I shan't give up. Leon has Sheena. They're together more and more often these days.'

'Yes, I know,' admitted Georgina. She had seen them and it was like someone turning a knife in her heart. No matter how often or how much she told herself it was madness to go on pining after him, her love would not go away. There were moments when she ached to touch him, ached for his kisses, but she had to hide it all beneath a mask of indifference, pretend she did not care. He had accepted the fact that she did not want an affair and so he had lost interest.

When she began to feel vaguely unwell Georgina thought it was because she wasn't eating properly, but as the days went by and her queasiness began to follow a regular pattern she knew what was wrong.

The thought that she was going to have Leon's baby both delighted and terrified her. She wanted to tell him but could not. She did not want him to feel obliged to marry her. It would be too much of a strain and the relationship would never work out. She did not tell Robert either; she told no one. This job would be finished long before she started to show and then she could go away and create a new life for herself. God worked in mysterious ways she thought. She could not have the man she loved but instead was being given his child. A tiny part of him to carry through the black days ahead.

It wasn't difficult to hide her sickness from Leon because he always breakfasted before her. One Sunday morning, however, they met in the kitchen and he looked at her sharply when she entered. 'You're looking peaky lately, Georgina. Aren't you sleeping well?'

'I'm all right,' she shrugged. 'A little tired, that's all.' And she slotted bread which she knew she would not eat into the toaster.

He continued to watch her, making her feel more and more uncomfortable, and when her toast was ready and buttered, and her coffee poured, she picked it up and headed for the door. 'Excuse me, I'll eat this in the studio. There's some work I want to finish.' Outside the kitchen door she took a couple of breaths to steady herself and then made her way upstairs.

The toast and coffee were still untouched when Leon walked into the room a quarter of an hour later. Georgina was sitting staring into space and did not hear him enter. When his hand touched her shoulder she almost jumped out of her skin.

'If it's so difficult for you, Georgina, living here with me, then don't feel you have to stay. You can go any time you like. And I don't mean to the cottage, I mean back home.' There was an inevitability to his tone. He knew it had come to the parting of the ways, he knew he was making her unhappy, though he would never know the real reason, and he was doing the decent thing and letting her go.

Georgina felt a lump as big as a golf ball in her throat and did not know how she stopped herself from crying. But weakness was one thing she had never shown in front of Leon and she had no intention of starting now. 'That's very kind of you.'

He had to bend his head to hear her words. 'I'm sorry, Georgina, I didn't mean to hurt you this much. I didn't realise that living with me was such a terrible strain.'

It's not, it's not, she wanted to cry out, it's not living with you, it's your attitude. Why can't you love me? Please, why? Why can't you forget what Anita did to you? Why can't you let yourself love again?

It was a long moment before she spoke, then she said softly. 'Thank you, Leon, I'd like to go. In any case I think I've done as much for you as I possibly can. Everything is ordered, everything is recorded; it should all fall into place.'

He still stood behind her, his hand heavy on her shoulder, and Georgina had to fight the urge to turn into his arms and feel his strength and warmth for one last time.

'Let me know when you're ready,' he said, 'and I'll arrange for my plane to fly you back.'

Georgina swallowed hard. This was it, then, the end. He had achieved his ultimate aim. This was what it had all been about. Not the baby, not that. He couldn't be blamed for that. She had been as guilty as he in wanting to make love. But her capitulation had been complete—and now he was no longer interested in her.

She did not say another word; she could not, she was too choked with emotion, and as the silence lengthened, the air heavy with thoughts and words unsaid, his fingers relaxed, until finally he let her go and strode from the room.

Two days later she was ready to leave. They had been two of the unhappiest days in her life. Thankfully Leon had kept out of her way as she finalised her work on the hotel, making sure there were no loose ends, and that when she had gone everything would run as smoothly as silk.

On the morning of her departure she took one last look around Stramore House. She would have liked to see the finished result, the culmination of all her weeks of hard work, but she had known what she was giving up when she'd grasped at the straw Leon offered. This was by far the best solution.

Leon was driving her to the airstrip despite her protests that she could go by taxi. He came to her room to pick up her case. 'Are you sure you know what you're doing, Georgina?'

Her heart lurched. 'Very sure.'

'If everything comes together as it should, and I have every faith that it will, then I'll be losing an excellent designer. I'm serious about buying a chain of hotels and I'd dearly love you to design their interiors.'

'I'm not the only designer in the world,' she said, feeling suddenly crushed. For just a moment, a crazy moment, she had thought he wanted her to stay for purely personal reasons. What an idiot she was.

'But you're the only Georgina. I'm going to miss you.'

I'll miss you too, she thought to herself.

'And there's so much we still have to talk about.'

She frowned. 'Such as what?'

'I want to be a part of your life, Georgina.' He spoke so softly that she only just caught his words. And then she thought she wasn't hearing him correctly.

'I beg your pardon?'

'Georgina, please, don't make this any harder for me. I know you don't love me but you can't deny that we're compatible—we proved that on the boat. I don't want you to go. I want you to stay with me. I think we could make a go of things, and, who knows, in time you might even——'

'Leon, what are you trying to tell me?' she cut in, her heart erupting into a frenzy of excitement.

'That I love you, you adorable creature.'

Leon loved her! She could not believe it. It was everything she had ever wanted.

'It's taken me a long time to feel like this again,' he went on, 'and it wasn't until you made up your mind to leave that I realised I couldn't face the thought of life without you. You mean so much to me, Georgina. Please stay. I want you to be my wife, I want you to marry me. I know I've been a swine, I readily admit it, but you can't walk out on me now. I love you. I've loved you from the first day we met.'

'You had a funny way of showing it,' she said, still hiding her delight.

'I was deeply hurt and disappointed when I thought you were a fortune-hunter.'

'But you cleared all that up when you sent for Craig. As a matter of fact I still don't know why you went to all that trouble. Why didn't you just phone him?'

'Because, Georgina, I wanted to see the two of you together. I wanted to check for myself what your feelings were for him.'

'And were you satisfied?'

He nodded. 'But by that time you'd made it very clear that you had no feelings for me, so I was afraid to tell you that I loved you. Afraid you might laugh in my face. Love needs to be a two-sided affair. It's my own fault, I know, I killed whatever affection you had for me in the beginning—I was even jealous of your own brother.'

'Ross?' she said. 'Yes. And I was jealous of that girl you were with. I'd been waiting for days for your phone call.'

His lips twisted wryly. 'That was purely business, nothing more. I'd planned to phone you the next day. God, I can't tell you how I felt when I saw you with him in that restaurant. It was as if the bottom had dropped out of my world. But please, don't go now. Please, Georgina, I'm begging you, stay. I'll make you love me, I will, I will. I'll——'

'There's no need, Leon,' cut in Georgina gently, her head filled with music as though all the angels in heaven were singing.

He frowned.

'I already love you,' she whispered shyly.

'You do?' He looked as though he found it impossible to believe.

'With all my heart, Leon. I always have.'

'But you said——'

'I was angry, angry and hurt. I thought you were playing about with me.'

'How about Robert?'

She shook her head. 'Robert is a friend, nothing more. He loves me, I'll admit that, but I don't feel anything for him.'

'Nor do I for Sheena,' he confessed quietly. 'She was a balm for my wounded pride, that is all. From the day I met you I wanted no other girl.'

'Oh, Leon!'

'Oh, Georgina, my darling Georgina.' At last he gathered her into his arms and kissed her, a kiss filled with the passion of a hungry man. Then he said, 'Is it true, is it really true that you love me?'

She nodded.

'You won't leave me?'

'No.'

'You'll marry me?'

With difficulty she swallowed the lump in her throat. 'I think we should, for the sake of our baby.'

She felt him freeze, his heart and pulse, everything stopped for a moment in time. Then his lips moved, although the words were soundless. 'Our baby?'

She nodded, full of her love now, not afraid to show it, proud she was bearing his child.

'Oh, my God, Georgina. You were going away without telling me? My child. I might never have known. Georgina, how could you do that to me?'

'Please, Leon, please, don't be upset. I thought it was for the best. I didn't know you loved me, and I thought that if I couldn't have you then your baby was the next best thing.'

He took her face into his hands and looked deeply into her eyes. 'What a mess we almost made of our lives, and I'm entirely to blame. I'll never be able to make it up to you, Georgina. Never.'

'Oh, my darling, please don't say that.' She put her hands over his. 'I think you'd have sought me out. You wouldn't have let me disappear completely out of my life, not if you love me as much as you say you do.'

He nodded. 'We both needed time to come to terms with our emotions, to decide which way our future lay.' He gently placed his hand over her stomach. 'Our child. Our child, Georgina. Born of our love for each other, though neither of us knew it at the time.'

'I don't know why you didn't guess,' she said. 'I gave you my all that night after the storm.'

'And then told me that it meant nothing to you.'

She pulled a rueful face. 'I had to protect myself.'

'And I had to take a cold shower to cool my ardour. I wanted you so much, Georgina. I couldn't believe that you didn't feel the same.'

'It hurt me,' she admitted. 'I didn't sleep a wink. I sat all night watching you, loving you, thinking about you, and the next morning you were cold and hard and I was glad I hadn't given myself to you again.'

'We've made some foolish mistakes,' he said. 'We have a lot of making up to do. I thought when I woke up this morning that this was going to be the saddest day of my life; instead it's turned out to be the happiest. I almost didn't tell you, do you know that? It took a lot of courage. Oh, my darling, I love you with all my heart, and I always will.'

'And I will always love you,' she promised. Their mouths met and it was their first kiss given in mutual love, it was a promise of things to come, it was sealing their new-found love for ever.

HARLEQUIN 🜂 PRESENTS®

BARBARY WHARF

**Home to the *Sentinel*
Home to passion, heartache and love**

Charlotte Lamb

The BARBARY WHARF six-book saga continues with Book Five, A SWEET ADDICTION. Guy Faulkner and Sophie Watson have both been abandoned by the people they love, but is that reason enough to find themselves in each other's arms? It isn't for Sophie. And it isn't the kind of solace Gina Tyrrell wants from Nick Caspian, either—despite the fact that she's becoming increasingly confused about her feelings for the tall, handsome man. But love them or leave them, these men just won't go away!

A SWEET ADDICTION (Harlequin Presents #1530) available in February.

HARLEQUIN®

my Valentine 1993

The most romantic day of the year is here! Escape into the exquisite world of love with MY VALENTINE 1993. What better way to celebrate Valentine's Day than with this very romantic, sensuous collection of four original short stories, written by some of Harlequin's most popular authors.

ANNE STUART
JUDITH ARNOLD
ANNE McALLISTER
LINDA RANDALL WISDOM

THIS VALENTINE'S DAY, DISCOVER ROMANCE
WITH MY VALENTINE 1993

Available in February wherever Harlequin Books are sold.

VAL93

HARLEQUIN PRESENTS®

A Year
DOWN UNDER

In February, we will take you to Sydney, Australia, with
NO GENTLE SEDUCTION by Helen Bianchin,
Harlequin Presents #1527.

Lexi Harrison and Georg Nicolaos move in the right
circles. Lexi's a model and Georg is a wealthy Sydney
businessman. Life seems perfect...so why have they
agreed to a *pretend* engagement?

Share the adventure—and the romance—
of A Year Down Under!

Available this month in
A YEAR DOWN UNDER

HEART OF THE OUTBACK
by Emma Darcy
Harlequin Presents #1519
Wherever Harlequin books are sold.   YDU-J